Disney
PIRATES of the CARIBBEAN

LEGENDS OF THE BRETHREN COURT

Rising in the East

Rob Kidd

Based on the earlier adventures of characters created
for the theatrical motion picture,
"Pirates of the Caribbean: The Curse of the Black Pearl"
Screen Story by Ted Elliott & Terry Rossio and
Stuart Beattie and Jay Wolpert,
Screenplay by Ted Elliott & Terry Rossio,
And characters created for the theatrical motion pictures
"Pirates of the Caribbean: Dead Man's Chest" and
"Pirates of the Caribbean: At World's End"
written by Ted Elliott & Terry Rossio

DISNEP PRESS

New York

DISNEYPIRATES.COM

PIRATES of the CARIBBEAN

LEGENDS OF THE
BRETHREN COURT

Rising in the East

PROLOGUE

*B*eware.

The bold, dark handwriting gleamed on the paper as if the ink were still fresh on the letter, although the message had traveled nearly halfway around the world.

We are all in grave danger.

A soft breeze wafted through the open window, carrying the distant scent of the ocean. Beyond it were the fish market, the brightly colored flowers in the trees outside, and the murmur of the city down the hill. The breeze lifted the paper a little, then darted away as if the contents had scared it off.

A new threat has arisen. A scourge worse than any pirate. He calls himself the Shadow Lord, and he commands a vast army capable of unspeakable horrors. We cannot even describe the scene of devastation we found in Panama . . . the brutality, the destruction, the waste—of life and property.

And it grows worse still. Our agents tell us he has formed an alliance with the Spanish—our mortal foes. Together, they plan to slaughter every pirate on the sea . . . and then turn on us.

Take heed, my good sir. Watch closely for any sign of this Shadow Lord. Warn us if you hear anything of him. The Company depends on our loyalty and strength. We must all be vigilant in this time of peril.

The letter was signed by a fellow employee of

the East India Trading Company, a man who had once served on a merchant ship with the recipient. The latter, a skeletal, fastidious, pale blond gentleman who now sat at his desk studying the letter through a monocle, had risen higher and faster in the Company than his friend had. If you asked the recipient, he would have said that was because he did not suffer from the flights of fancy, ridiculous fears, and soft-hearted sentimentality that the letter-writer clearly displayed in his melodramatic tale of horror.

This man with the monocle was Benedict Huntington, and he was manager, lord, and chief of all business appertaining to the East India Trading Company on the very profitable island of Hong Kong and its surrounding seas. How profitable? Huntington's mansion reveals that: set high above the bustle and smells of the city, surrounded by lavish gardens, elaborately furnished and decorated with the most expensive silks and treasures of the Far East. Or perhaps the entourage of fifty servants that attend to his every whim might paint a clear picture of just how vast his riches are. Perhaps you could guess at his wealth from the fawning looks he gets from every other Englishman in the city, or by the heavy jewels adorning his strikingly beautiful young wife.

Benedict slid the letter under a book as his wife, Barbara Huntington, swept into the room. But Barbara's sharp green eyes spotted the movement instantly. She pounced.

"What's that?"

"Nothing to trouble yourself with, my dear—" Benedict began, but Barbara was already perching on the edge of the desk and yanking the letter out from under the book. Her unnaturally bright red locks were pinned back with an enormous peacock feather that swooped out of the top of her hair, and Benedict had the uneasy feeling that the eyes on the feather looming over him were staring at him disapprovingly. Barbara's long silk gown matched the brilliant blues and greens of the feather, and strings of emeralds dripped from her ears, wrists, and neck.

People who met the couple couldn't help wondering if the wife had drained all the color out of her husband upon marrying him. She was dazzling, like a startling bird flashing out amid the jungle foliage, while he would be easy to lose in a mild snow flurry. His hair was so pale it was nearly white. Even his eyebrows and eyelashes, perched above nearly colorless light blue eyes, barely made an appearance on his bony face. He was partial to wearing entirely white suits, with white stockings and shoes and a wide-brimmed white hat to protect him from the sun, which he seemed to loathe, as he avoided it with the same cautious, austere intensity that he devoted to his business affairs, wardrobe, and all his habits.

Where his wife was loud and vivacious, he was quiet and calculating. Many a diplomat had found himself distracted by the charms of one member of the couple, only to discover later that the other had weaseled some vital secret out of him without his noticing it.

"What rubbish," Barbara said, tossing the letter back on the desk. "A Shadow Lord indeed! Someone has been reading too many ghost stories, don't you think, Benny?"

"As I said," her husband replied calmly, "nothing worth your attention."

"Well, I don't know." Barbara examined her nails, painted the same fiery red as her hair. "Perhaps we can use this to our advantage in some way. Terrified bureaucrats are so easy to manipulate. We could give the Company higher-ups a little kick in the knickers—maybe expand your position to encompass the entire Pacific Ocean. Wouldn't that be thrilling, dear? Or maybe we should make a deal with this 'Shadow Lord' ourselves! Ridding the sea of those flea-bitten pirates sounds like a brilliant idea to me."

Their eyes narrowed simultaneously, and anyone watching would have been struck by the sudden similarity in their faces—the cunning ferocity that had drawn them to each other despite their outward differences.

"Another ship yesterday," Benedict hissed. "Lost with all its cargo, probably never to be seen again."

"I *hate* that insipid Mistress Ching!" Barbara said violently, jumping to her feet and stamping her foot. "There was a wondrous selection of tea and spices coming to me from Shanghai and she *co-opted* it. Oh, Benny, we must catch her and have her hanged. Does she not know that the world belongs to the East India Trading Com-pany? Or, worse, does she know and choose to ignore the fact?" Barbara inhaled some snuff, patted her hair, and wiped her nose.

"I will catch her," Benedict said in a voice that was as soft and sickening as opium smoke. "Shadow Lords and Spanish armies—their kind means nothing to us. Someone else can deal with them back in their own waters; we have more pressing troubles. I assure you, darling, sooner or later, that pirate woman will be at our mercy."

"And then *I* want to kill her," Barbara snarled. "I'll tighten the noose around her neck myself. That'll teach her—teach them all—to steal my things. She and every other pirate should be twitching at the end of a rope somewhere on the Seven Seas."

"Yes, *every* one," Benedict said, touching his long white fingers together. "And that is where they will all be . . . before long."

Barbara patted her hair again and smiled dazzlingly. "Thank you, darling. I knew you would have a plan."

CHAPTER ONE

"**I** knew you didn't have a plan, Jaaaaack!" Hector Barbossa bellowed. "Ye barely even know which end of the ship is up! I bet you've never read a chart in your whole misbegotten, pernicious, confounding—" The rest of his words were (perhaps mercifully) lost in a deluge of water as enormous waves swept over the side of the *Black Pearl*, leaving Barbossa, her first mate, clutching his hat and sputtering.

"What? Eh?" said Captain Jack Sparrow from the helm, cupping his hand around his ear. "Did you hear something?" Jack asked Diego, his kohl-rimmed eyes darting from side to side as if there might be sprites talking in the air all around him. Then he winked at Diego. "Must have been the wind, eh?"

A howling gale raged around the *Black Pearl*, trying with furious force to smash her against the rocks of the Strait of Magellan. Rain lashed the sails and drenched the poor souls on deck, while an icy wind off the South Pole chilled them all to the bone.

The ship had been trapped in what seemed like an endless storm for three days straight as they navigated around the tip of South America, heading for the Pacific Ocean. "Go that way" seemed like a perfectly reasonable plan to Jack. He didn't know what Barbossa was on about—but Barbossa was always grumbling about something, so Jack had learned not to pay much attention.

Diego was too cold to answer Jack. He had never been so cold, not even when he was a young boy sleeping in the stables in the depths of Spain's winter. He wanted to be a good, useful sailor, but his teeth chattered as he clung to the mast and he couldn't feel his fingers or toes anymore. When he saw a slim figure emerge from the hatch, he let go and slid over to her. His shoes slipped and splashed on the soaking deck.

"Carolina!" he yelled over the roar of the storm. "Get back down below! It's too dangerous up here!"

"So why are you out here?" she shouted back. The rain plastered her tunic and trousers to her body instantly despite her long cloak, which was less of a shield and more of a plaything for the wind. Carolina grabbed the edges of the cloak to make sure it didn't fly away, perhaps even taking her with it. "It's just as dangerous for you as it is for me!" she challenged Diego.

"Well—but—but I'm not a princess!" he answered. From the flash of her dark eyes, he knew he'd said the wrong thing.

"I'm not a princess anymore, either!" Carolina snapped, her long dark hair flying wetly around her shoulders. "I'm a pirate now! And if you think I'm just some weak, simpering child of royalty who has to be pampered, I dare you to race me to the bird's nest and we'll just see who's the better sailor!"

Diego felt sick at the thought of climbing the ratlines in this weather. "No, no!" he cried. "That's not what I meant! You're a much better sailor than me! It's not that you're weak—I meant that you're more important than I am!"

The ship heaved to one side, tossing Carolina into Diego's arms as they both stumbled on the slippery deck. He shivered at the nearness of her soft skin and scented hair. "Oh, you are cold," Carolina said, instinctively putting her hands under his shirt to warm him up. He jumped, startled, and to his regret she pulled away, looking embarrassed.

"You have to stop thinking of me as being more important than you," Carolina said, leaning close to him so she didn't have to shout. "We're the same now. Just two pirates aboard Captain Jack Sparrow's ship."

Diego all but ignored her. He tried to stand in a way that would shield Carolina from the bitter wind. The rain lashed against his back.

"Besides," Carolina added, "I couldn't stay below for one more minute. I'd rather be out here in the pouring rain than stuck down there with your 'bonnie lass,' as Captain Sparrow calls her."

"She's not my bonnie lass!" Diego protested. "Stop saying that! She might hear you!"

"Oooooo, *Diego*," Carolina twittered in a perfect imitation of Marcella, the bonnie lass in question. "You're my *hero*, Diego. You're so *smart*, Diego. Take off your *shirt*, Diego."

"Carolina!"

"Oh, calm down," Carolina said with a smile.

Neither of them spotted the glimmer of lamplight through the grating over the hatchway below, where another figure was crouched, listening intently. Marcella's eyes narrowed as she drew back further into the shadows. She could only catch a few words through the storm—but she'd heard enough to be sure that Carolina was making fun of her. That Spanish ragamuffin trying to poison Diego against her! Marcella clenched her fists, wondering if anyone would notice if Carolina "accidentally" fell overboard during the storm. But to do that Marcella would probably have to get wet, and Marcella hated getting wet with a strange, fiery passion.

She absolutely refused to go on deck in this weather, no matter who cajoled or entreated her.

"Marcella? What are you doing there?" Jean Magliore, Marcella's cousin, said as he emerged from the crew's quarters, his reddish hair standing up in sleepy tufts.

"Nothing," Marcella snapped. "I don't understand how you can sleep in this horrible boat, with all these horrible smells and all this horrible noise and everything flying around everywhere. I nearly had a barrel fall on me earlier! A whole barrel full of those nasty biscuits they think we're going to eat!"

Jean hid a smile and tried to nod comfortingly.

"And there's no one else down here," Marcella went on, "so you don't have to call me Marcella—which is a stupid name, by the way—"

Jean jumped forward and covered her mouth with his hand. "Shhhh!" he said frantically. He peered around at the flickering shadows belowdecks. "I told you not to talk about that," he whispered. "If Jack finds out who you are, he'll throw us both off the ship, and he won't care if we're in the middle of the Pacific Ocean when he does it!"

Marcella shoved his hand away. "Well, I think that's just rude!" she said.

Just then, Jack flounced by.

"All right, Marcella," Jean said loudly, "why don't we go find out what's for dinner?"

Marcella rolled her eyes and stormed ahead of him toward the galley.

"I *know* what's for dinner," she sniped at top volume. "Something *truly horrible* with a side of something very nasty, plus a 'biscuit' with all the flavor and texture of a New Orleans cobblestone."

Jean glanced around nervously one more time and then followed her. He tried not to look straight at any of the hanging lanterns, which

16

were swinging madly as the ship bounced over the waves. Marcella was one of the few who had not been affected at all by seasickness during this storm. Somehow she was still able to eat astonishing amounts of food, complaining vigorously over every bite.

Unfortunately for the rest of the crew, Marcella did have a point. The situation in the galley had deteriorated rapidly after the *Pearl*'s cook, Gombo, had gone off to captain his own pirate ship as Gentleman Jocard. While the *Pearl* had been sailing south along the coast of Argentina, the pirates had gone ashore several times for fruit, but now it had been days since their last landfall, and the remaining food supplies did not look very appetizing.

Billy Turner was sitting at the long table in the galley with his head in his hands. Jack had lured him onto the *Black Pearl* with the promise that he would take Billy straight back to his family in North Carolina. But Billy should have known better than to believe anything Jack said. Now he was trapped on this mad expedition to Asia, with no prospect of getting home anytime soon.

After a brief encounter with the creepiest mystic in the Caribbean, Tia Dalma, Jack was on a mission to collect vials of Shadow Gold to defeat the Shadow Lord and his Shadow Army,* whatever that was all about, and Billy was fairly certain he was stuck on this ship at least until the Shadow Gold was found. At *least.*

The vials of Shadow Gold Jack was looking for had been scattered by Tia Dalma's zombie, Alex, and they were now being held by five of the nine Pirate Lords around the world. The problem was figuring out *which* Pirate Lords had them. Jack had run into the Spanish Pirate

* As detailed in Vol. 1, *The Caribbean.*

Lord, Villanueva, while Jack was liberating a wayward vial from the Incas. So now Jack knew two things: Villanueva did not have a vial. And, according to the rumors, Mistress Ching—Pirate Lord of the Pacific Ocean, based in China—did. That was enough for Jack.

"Cheer up, Billy," Jean said, clapping him on the shoulder. "Just think, we're going to Asia! We're going to see Shanghai and Hong Kong and Singapore again—and who knows what else!"

"I *know* what else," Billy said gloomily. "Lots of water. Lots of angry pirates. Lots of swords in our faces. It won't be any different than the last time we were there."

"Why, you don't think Mistress Ching will just hand over her vial of Shadow Gold?" Jean said with a cheerful grin.. "Jack is *très bon* at persuasion, after all."

Billy snorted. "Perchance you're forgetting

the last few times Jack has tried to charm some-body into doing what he wants."

"He charmed you onto this ship, didn't he, *mon ami*?" Jean winked.

Billy grimaced.

"I'm not eating *this*," Marcella interrupted, slamming a hardtack biscuit down on the table. The biscuits were round and sturdy and could last for months. They were baked ahead of time exactly for a trip like this. In fact, as far as Jean could tell, these biscuits already had lasted for months. Possibly years. Maybe . . . centuries?

Marcella repeatedly banged the biscuit against the side of the table. It went CLONK, CLONK, CLONK, like a hammer against a nail. Not even a crumb fell off. The biscuits were called "hardtack" for a reason.

"I'm not breaking my perfect teeth on something this horrible," Marcella said. ("Perfect" was a bit of a stretch, Billy thought.

In truth, Marcella's teeth were a bit yellow, a bit crooked, and surprisingly small.) "And I'm not eating *that*, whatever it is," she went on, pointing to a barrel of dried salt pork that looked orange and wrinkled and flaky. "And I'm definitely not eating *these* nasty things." She ran her fingers through a barrel of shriveled brown peas and shuddered.

"You miss Gombo, don't you?" Jean said.

"I most certainly do not," Marcella said, throwing her shoulders back and crossing her arms. "That ungrateful, self-centered wretch just sailed away without even a good-bye. Leaving us with no cook at all! He didn't spend even one second thinking of what would happen to the rest of us! He's just a stupid, dreadful *pirate*. I don't care if I never see him again!" She tossed her stringy hair.

Jean looked at her closely. Were those . . . tears in her eyes?

BOOM!

A muffled sound, like faraway thunder, echoed through the ship. Jean and Billy exchanged worried glances. Surely that wasn't—

BOOM!

The ship rocked as if something heavy had just landed in the water beside it.

Something like a cannonball.

"Anyway, he never cooked my fish as rare as I like it, and he was all big and muscley and— hey!" Marcella realized that Billy and Jean had raced away to the deck. "I was *talking*, people!" she fumed. "Pirates!" She threw the biscuit at the wall. It bounced off and hit the floor with a dull, unappetizing thud.

Jean poked his head through the hatch and realized that the storm was finally dying down. The heavy rain had become a light shower, tapping gently on the boards of the deck. The cold wind still whistled through the black sails, but something much more urgent than the thunderstorm had appeared on the horizon.

Two ships were bearing down on the *Black Pearl* with frightening speed. It was as if they had hidden behind the thunderclouds, lying in wait until the *Pearl* reached the end of the strait and came upon the open waters of the Pacific Ocean.

Even through the rain, Jack recognized the winglike shape of the red sails, the sleek outline of the ships, and the bright crimson banners fluttering from the masts. He snapped his spyglass shut. These were Chinese pirate junks, a type of ship known throughout the world for its speed and maneuverability. But here? At the gateway to the Pacific, just off the South American coast? It was clear that someone did not want the *Pearl* to enter the Pacific Ocean, and Jack had a good idea who that might be.

If there were ever a time for the *Pearl*'s

legendary swiftness to be tested, this was it! But first they had to get around the junks, which were planted directly in their path.

Jack narrowed his eyes and opened his mouth to speak.

"Mistress Ching," Barbossa muttered darkly.

"Hey, I was about to say that!" Jack objected. "I even had an excessively ominous tone of voice prepared. Quite better than your own, actually. Here, listen: 'Mistress Ching,'" he intoned, pitching his voice as low as possible and drawing the words out slowly. "See? You're not the only one who can do that whole sinister, brooding thing." He waved his hand up and down as if summing up Barbossa.

"Jack, this is no time for your strange behavior," Barbossa snarled. "Mistress Ching's ships will blow us out of the water in a matter of moments."

"Captain, Captain, *Captain* Jack, my dear

Hector. *Captain* Jack," Jack reminded him with an unruffled smile. He wasn't worried. The effects of the second vial of Shadow Gold, which he had poured down his throat on top of a mountain in South America, were still coursing through his veins.* He felt strong and alive and full of a powerful energy, like he could almost go running across the water to kick in the sides of those ships if he wanted to. That's what the Shadow Gold did. It wasn't valued as a precious metal, but as a liquid amalgamation that could restore youth to the person who consumed it.

It also was a cure for the heavy shadow-sickness that had plagued Jack since Tortuga—a shadow-sickness that only all seven vials of Shadow Gold could cure. That was what Tia Dalma had told him. But Jack had decided it best not to share all that information with his

---

*Jack gulped down the second vial in Vol. 1, *The Caribbean*.

crew. They might take it amiss that they were sailing all the way around the world just to save Jack's life. They were pirates, after all. Selfish, the lot of them.

So, instead, the crew thought Jack was on a mission to find the gold and stop the Shadow Lord. Some of them seemed to have the distinct impression that they would be sharing the wealth that would come from selling the Shadow Gold in the end. Jack wasn't sure where they'd gotten that idea. Surely not from anything he'd said. Certainly not.

And, of course, he didn't let any of the others know that drinking the gold would have any affect at all.

"Is that Mistress Ching herself?" Carolina asked excitedly, running to the front railing. "Are we going to see her?" Beside her, Diego shivered, remembering the tales he'd heard of the fearsome Chinese Pirate Lord.

"You mean, see her *laughing* as our ship goes down in flames?" Billy said, joining the group around the steering wheel. "That *does* sound like something to look forward to."

"Always so negative, mate," Jack said, cocking his hat blithely. "We haven't met a ship yet that can outrun the *Black Pearl*."

"Of course you would want to run," Barbossa growled.

"And no," Jack said, ignoring his first mate, "I doubt very much that the notorious Mistress Ching would come sailing all the way over here just to fight off a couple of measly intruders in her territory. Of course, if she knew it were Captain Jack Sparrow, I'm sure she'd have made an exception."

"Oh, yes," Barbossa said, rolling his eyes. "I wager she's quaking in her slippers at the very thought."

"Mistress Ching commands a fleet of thousands

of these junks," Billy said to Carolina, pointing at the approaching ships. "She can spare a few to guard this entrance to her territory. They probably have orders to loot any merchant ship that comes this way and drive off rival pirates. Say, Jack, you know where there *wouldn't* be any pirate junks, Jack? NORTH CAROLINA."

"Sorry, Billy, mate, I'd love to chat about that, but I've got to concentrate here," Jack said, furrowing his brow and focusing closely on steering.

The *Pearl* swerved to the right just as another cannonball whistled past the masts and landed with a splash. Now the ships were close enough for the *Pearl*'s crew to see the eyes painted on the bows and the elaborate dragon heads at the ends of the cannons. A couple of them were still smoking, as if the dragons were alive and breathing fire.

"Ahoy!" Jack shouted at the ships. "Lovely day,

isn't it? Just passing through! No need to poke any holes in anyone's ships, most especially mine!"

BOOM! responded the nearest ship. This cannonball landed close enough to swamp the deck with a wave of water.

"OI!" Jack bellowed, waving his arms. Alex, the zombie that Tia Dalma had given Jack to be her eyes and ears on the ship, shuffled up behind him, squelching wetly.

"Stop that!" Jack yelled indignantly out to sea toward the junks. "We're not here to steal your plunder! And we've got no loot for you, either! Not even any rum! I don't know why, but the rum's always gone! So, really, no need for this unnecessary violence—nothing at all to steal!"

"Except for—" Alex began, and both Jack and Billy kicked the zombie in the shins. There was an unfortunate squishing sound and Jack made a face as he realized there were bits of decaying Alex-leg left on his boot.

Jack could see the sailors on the attacking ships running around to reload the dragon-headed cannons. Still attacking. And here Jack was, being perfectly reasonable for once!

"I don't think they care about your plunder, Jack," Barbossa pointed out. "All they want is to drive anyone out of Mistress Ching's territory."

"Don't care about plunder!" Jack cried. "Some beastie has addled those pirates' brains."

"Whatever the reason," Billy said, pulling out his pistols, "it looks like we have no choice. We have to fight."

CHAPTER TWO

"To the cannons!" Jack bellowed. "Battle stations! About the sails! Man the jib or the foresail or whatever it is! Just point some guns at those ships and shoot!"

"Remember, lads . . ." Barbossa shouted. Carolina shot him a nasty look. ". . . and lasses," Barbossa added. "If we don't get past these ships, it's back into the strait for us, and another few weeks of nothing but hardtack to eat!"

That got everyone moving. The crew scurried madly around the deck, loading cannons and trimming sails. One pirate came staggering up from below and promptly tripped over his boots, tumbling across the boards and taking down three other pirates as he rolled. It was Catastrophe Shane. He was truly a disaster . . . even among a crew as haphazard as the *Pearl*'s.

"Diego!" Jack shouted, pointing at the heap of men. "Grab Shane! Make sure he's not underfoot!"

Diego leaped down to the deck, untangled the accident-prone pirate from his shipmates, and led him over to one of the masts. Resigned, Shane sat down and let Diego tie him up, so he would be out of the way and out of trouble.

BLAM! BLAM!

Jack jumped, startled. Turning, he saw that Carolina had liberated a pistol from his belt and was aiming at the nearest Chinese ship. He checked his pockets to make sure nothing else was missing.

"Look here, love," he said, reaching gingerly for the gun, "I really think I should be the one holding the—"

BLAM! BLAM!

Jack threw himself to the deck. But through the railing he saw that Carolina had fired right into the mouths of the junk's cannons. Now sailors on the other ship were scattering away from the cannon as fast as they could.

With an enormous bang, the two cannons exploded backward, sending iron pieces flying across the deck of the junk and leaving giant holes in the side of the ship.

Jack made a face. He didn't like it when other people had clever ideas. On the other hand, he *did* like it when his ship didn't have great big holes in it. Quickly he jumped to his feet and ran to the wheel. He steered the *Black Pearl* behind the broken ship, placing the wounded junk between the *Pearl* and the other pirate ship. Now the second Chinese junk couldn't fire on the *Pearl* without hitting its comrade. That gave the *Pearl* just enough time to scoot around the ships and make it to open water.

A brisk wind immediately filled the *Pearl*'s black sails. Waving his hat cheerfully at the defeated junks, Jack sailed his ship away at top speed, knowing that there was no chance the *Pearl* could be caught now.

The crew breathed a collective sigh of relief as the burning junk grew smaller on the horizon behind them.

Now all that stood between Jack and Mistress Ching's vial of Shadow Gold was the Pacific Ocean. And a few hundred other pirate junks. And the twisted, dangerous streets of Shanghai. And the Pirate Lord's personal coterie of fearsome, trained-assassin bodyguards.

But other than that—nothing to worry about.

"**D**ieeeeeeeeeeeeeeeeeeeeeeeeeeeeeeeeeeeeeeeego! Oh, Dieeeeeeeeeeeeeeeeeeeeeeeeeego!"

Diego looked around the deck frantically. There was nowhere to hide. Marcella was hunting for him, and if he didn't escape soon he would find himself rehanging her hammock (again) or showing her how to make tea (again) or listening to endless stories about her various ailments, sore feet, muddy dresses, and all the other pains and horrors she had to endure on this "nasty ship." For some reason unknown to him, Marcella had decided that he was the only one who really "listened" to her. Diego had no idea how he had made such a terrible error. Or how the pained expression of terror and suffering on his face could be mistaken for "listening."

"Diego, where *are* you?" Marcella's voice was getting closer. Soon she would come up the ladder to the deck and spot him. Diego lunged for the nearest ratline and started climbing. The crow's nest was a fairly depressing place to be in the middle of the vast, empty Pacific Ocean, but at least it was somewhere Marcella would never go. Once she had climbed a couple of feet up the ropes to prove that she was as good as Carolina, but then she panicked, froze, and had to be rescued—by Diego, of course. Climbing up was apparently not a problem for Marcella; but climbing back down was. So the higher he was, the safer he was.

Because no one else really wanted to sit up in the crow's nest, waiting for a Chinese junk to pop up on the horizon, and also because it kept his smell well away from the rest of the crew, Alex the zombie had been posted up at the crow's nest for the last three days. He didn't need to come down for food and water, so it was a perfect assignment. Jack kept wondering aloud why he hadn't thought of it sooner.

The zombie was staring blankly out to sea when Diego hauled himself over the edge of the basket. A whiff of decay hit Diego's nose, and he wondered whether this was really his best option. But when he glanced down and saw Marcella stomping angrily around the deck, he decided he should stay up here at least until dinner. That was, if he still had an appetite.

"*Hola*, Alex," Diego said nervously. "Er— how are you?"

Alex blinked at him as if this was a very odd question. But considering that Alex's eyeballs kind of rolled loosely around in his head, it was rather hard to tell what his facial expression was supposed to convey.

"Seen anything interesting?" Diego asked politely.

"No."

"Ah," Diego said. "Okay, then." He rubbed his arms to keep warm, trying to stay as far away as possible from the zombie, which was difficult in the tiny basket. All around them the sea sparkled blue and green like the jewels that Carolina used to wear in her former life as a princess. There was nothing to see for miles in any direction.

Unless . . .

Was that . . . ?

Diego squinted, shading his eyes from the sun. "Hey, Alex, do you see that?" he asked, pointing at a dark spot in the distance.

"Hey, Diego, no, I do not see that," Alex said in a monotone.

It was a little unsettling that the zombie knew his name. It was a lot unsettling that he couldn't see what Diego was pointing at. Maybe having reanimated dead-eyes wasn't so useful for someone in a crow's nest. Perhaps he wasn't such a perfect lookout after all.

Diego stared for a while until he was sure. There was definitely something out there. He memorized the direction.

"I'll go tell Jack," he said, climbing out of the basket.

"*Captain* Jack Sparrow," Alex said agreeably.

Diego sped down the ratlines, but before he could sprint across the deck to the captain's cabin, someone seized his arm in a startlingly strong grip.

"*There* you are!" Marcella cried triumphantly. "I was just saying, if only Diego were here, he'd understand why I can't eat any of those horrible biscuits and he'd catch me a fish for dinner instead. Won't you, wonderful Diego, please, please, please?" She batted her eyelashes at him, drawing attention to her strange yellow-brown eyes.

"I have to talk to Captain Jack," Diego said, prying her fingers off his arm.

"I'll come with you," she said, latching on even tighter. He sighed, dragged her over to the captain's cabin, and knocked.

"Nobody here!" Jack's voice called. "Very busy! I mean empty! Come back later! Or don't, that's all right, too!"

"Jack, I think I saw an island," Diego called through the door.

Immediately the door was flung open. Captain Sparrow stood there, his kohl-rimmed eyes wide. They widened even further when he saw Marcella, but before he could slam the door again, she shoved her way inside and threw herself down on the couch.

"Oh, lovely," Jack said with an insincere smile. "Just the visitor I was hoping for."

Marcella stuck out her tongue at him. She kicked off her shoes and put her feet up on the couch, fanning herself with her hand.

"I'm sure it's an island," Diego said. He pointed in the direction of the shape he'd seen. "Maybe we could resupply there."

"Darling Diego," Marcella said. "Always thinking of my comfort. I would *love* some fruit. And some water that doesn't taste like it has been sitting in a barrel for ten years. And some chocolate. Do you think they'll have chocolate on this island?" She stretched, yawning.

Jack leaned over the map on his desk. He narrowed his eyes and stared at it thoughtfully for a long time. Finally Diego pointed over his shoulder.

"Maybe it's that island?" Diego suggested.

"Oh, we're in *that* ocean!" Jack said. "No wonder I'm confused." He caught a movement out of the corner of his eye and glanced at Marcella wearily. She just blinked her peculiar yellow eyes at him, and he looked back down at the map.

" 'Rapa Nui,' " he read. " 'Also known as Easter

Island.' Well, that sounds cheerful! Much better than Quicksand Swamp Island or Horrible, Painful Death Island. Wonder if there will be bunnies and baskets. Oh! And eggs! How I do love a good egg."

The crew was quick to steer the ship toward the distant island, but as the *Pearl* sailed closer to the shore, an ominous silence drifted across the deck. Pirates gathered at the portside railing, staring at the strange sight.

"What is it?" Carolina whispered to Diego, standing on her tiptoes to see over the heads in front of her.

"Yeah, Diego, what is it?" Marcella said quickly from his other side, also standing on her tiptoes while clutching his arm for balance.

"I don't know," he said in awe.

Enormous stone heads peered out from the top of the cliff walls, glaring down at the *Black Pearl* as the ship sailed up to the island. Large hollow eyes seemed to follow their every move, hulking silently at the water's edge or looming from the rock faces far above them. They were taller than any man, vast and silent and mighty. What strange people had built these heads? For what purpose? Or were they once giants who lived here, transformed into rock by some supernatural power?

Even Jack couldn't hide a small shudder. But he was the captain and couldn't show fear. Besides, what harm could a bunch of stone heads really do?

"Right," he said. "Doesn't seem very Eastery, does it? Are you sure there wasn't a Halloweeny Island on that map? Maybe Big Stone Head Island?" He squinted at the shoreline. "Bit of an eerie welcoming party, but I wager they're great conversationalists. Who wants to go ashore and make some lovely, big, thickheaded friends?" No one volunteered right away. In fact, most of the crew shuffled around, trying to blend in with the scenery.

Jack pointed to Barbossa and Jean. "You two, come with me," he said. The first mate sighed and rolled his eyes. "Who else?"

"I'll go," said Carolina.

Diego said, "I'll go, too."

And immediately Marcella chimed in: "Me, too! I'll go, too!"

"Eeuuuugh," Jack said, peering at her with a skeptical expression. "Are you sure? There could be all sorts of beasties over there. Cannibals! Giant man-eating apes! Mosquitoes!"

"I want to go with Diego," Marcella insisted.

"Can I un-volunteer myself?" Barbossa wanted to know.

After some more bickering, during which Barbossa's request was pointedly ignored, the six of them finally got into one of the *Pearl*'s dinghies and headed for shore. It was a strange island; craggy mountains dominated the landscape, but there was hardly a tree in sight. Instead, rolling grassland surrounded the giant heads, stretching up the mountain slopes and off into the distance along the shore.

Diego and Jean rowed the small boat to the nearest beach and pulled it up on the sand. Marcella refused to get out until the boat was well out of the water, so this was a rather difficult task.

"I wouldn't want to get my *feet* wet!" she said in horror. "But if you want to carry me, Diego, that would be all right." She fluttered her eyelashes at him.

Diego gave an almighty heave, and the boat slid up out of the water. Carolina hid a smile. Disappointed, Marcella climbed out of the boat and immediately began complaining about the sand that had soiled her dress.

"It's so *sandy* here," she whined. "Ew, it's

getting into my *shoes*. Diego, can't you carry me up to the trees?"

"Marcella, come on," Jean said, embarrassed.

"Don't you *Marcella* me," his cousin snapped.

"It's too late now," Carolina said. "You're already sandy, you might as well stay that way and spare poor Diego's back."

Marcella drew herself up tall. "It's all right for those who don't *care* about their personal hygiene," she sniffed. "If some girls *want* to look like raggedy heathens, they're welcome to roll around in the dirt for all I care."

"Trap. Shut. Now," Jack said, ignoring Marcella's offended expression. "That small grove of trees in the distance seems like as good a place as any to look for water." He hurried up the beach to where the sand turned to grass, leaving the squabbling crew behind him.

Wide stretches of yellow-green grass swept out flatly ahead of them, all the way up the hills in the distance, leaving a clear line of sight for the row of giant heads ranged across the open plain. Jack didn't want to admit it, but another reason he wanted to head for the trees was to get to a place where the heads couldn't see him anymore. Not that they could really be staring at him . . . but it sure felt like it.

When they reached the trees they found a sparse grove of mostly palms, tall and creaking in the wind. It was cooler under their wide, jagged leaves, and the crewmates could hear the murmur of a stream. After only a few minutes of hiking, they came to a bubbling freshwater stream that ran down from the cliff above. Diego, Jean, and Barbossa knelt to fill their flasks while Carolina searched the ground for fallen coconuts. Jack, of course, supervised.

Marcella plunked herself down on a rock in the shade, ripped a large leaf off the nearest palm tree, and began fanning herself furiously.

"I *do* think," she said, "that *some* people ought to be *more respectful* of the fact that there is a *lady* aboard this ship, and I do mean *one* lady, who should be *treated* like the *delicate flower* that sheeeeeeeEEEEEEEEEEEEEEEEE!!!!!!!!!!"

For a moment, none of the others realized that the high-pitched scream wasn't just part of Marcella's regular complaining. But finally, Jack looked over and saw what was really happening.

A band of tattooed islanders had popped out from behind the tall palms. Now, several of them were winding vines around Marcella at lightning speed, while others lifted her over their heads. They dashed away through the trees, wearing green and brown so they blended into the landscape.

In the blink of an eye, Marcella was completely gone. Completely, that is, with the exception of her screaming, which could be heard echoing far behind her.

CHAPTER THREE

There was a shocked pause as everyone stared, frozen, at the spot where Marcella had been. Jack recovered first.

"Brilliant!" he cried. "Quick, back to the ship, before they change their minds!"

"Marcella!" Jean shouted. "Marcella, we'll rescue you, don't worry!"

"We will?" Jack asked. "Do we have to? Tell you what, why don't we come back for her later on? I suggest *after* we've sailed around the world and accomplished our mission. Maybe when we're very old and very deaf. Savvy?"

"I can't believe I'm saying this," Barbossa interjected, "but I agree with Jack." He made a face as if that notion made him ill. "Leave the lass here. She's no use on the *Pearl*."

"Jack, they could be cannibals!" Jean said desperately. "They could be taking her away to eat her! We don't know anything about these people!"

Jack stopped to think wistfully about how useful it would be if someone would just pop Marcella in a stew pot. But then Jean would probably sulk all the way back to the Caribbean, and nobody needed a pouting Creole sailor moping around the deck. Plus, Jack would love nothing more than to assert himself and go against Barbossa's will.

"All right," he said with a sigh. "Let's go after

her. Maybe she'll decide she wants to stay here," he added hopefully.

This hope of Jack's certainly didn't seem to be the case from Marcella's loud, piercing shrieks, which they could still hear. The good news (or bad, as Jack saw it) was that this made it quite easy to follow the islanders out of the trees to the grassland beyond. All they had to do was follow the sound of Marcella's voice.

"Those are some powerful lungs," Carolina said, impressed with Marcella for the first time.

"I think she sounds delighted," Jack said to Jean. "Try listening really closely—can't you hear? 'This is wonderful! I love this island! Leave me here!'" He checked Jean's stubborn expression hopefully. "Don't you hear it? I really think that's what she's saying, er, screaming."

"Over there!" Jean said, pointing to a thin column of smoke near the row of giant heads. "Quick, hurry!"

"Leeeeeeeeeeeeeeeave me!" Jack tried again, imitating Marcella's high-pitched shriek. "I love it heeeeeeeeeeeeeeere!"

But Jean was already running as fast as he could. With a sigh, Jack ran after him, and all the others came hurrying, too.

They raced across the open grass, heads in the process getting closer and closer to the enigmatic stone. They didn't look any friendlier—or smaller—up close. Jack realized there was a small village of thatched huts behind them; the smoke was rising from a few small cooking fires outside the doors. The islanders had dumped Marcella on the ground next to one of the heads and seemed to be having an argument in their own language. A new islander was standing with them, this one wearing a crown of tall feathers. Tattoos covered his whole body. He had his arms crossed, and he did not look pleased.

Marcella was lying on her side, still tied up with vines. And she was still screaming, one long, continuous, ear-bending shriek.

"Marcella!" Jean yelled.

Her eyes popped open and her mouth shut. All the islanders seemed to heave a huge sigh of relief. Their faces, as they turned toward Jack and the others, were much less hostile than Jack would have expected from folks who had just run off with a crew member.

"Diego!" Marcella cried. "I knew you would save me!" She tried to stand up, wobbled wildly as the vines restricted her, and then toppled to the ground face first with a crash.

The man with the crown stepped between Marcella and the pirates. He drew himself up very tall and frowned down at them. His large nose and big, dark eyes made him look strikingly like the huge stone head that was planted in the ground next to him. Jack glanced up at the looming, inanimate face and sidled away from it. Even if it was just a pile of rock . . . there was no need to draw its attention.

"Prisoner," the chief said shortly, pointing to Marcella, whose outrage was now muffled by her face being planted in the dirt.

"So we see," Jack said, twisting one of the braids in his beard. He lifted an eyebrow at Marcella as if she were an exotic bug that had turned up in his tea.

"Give her back!" Jean demanded.

"*Or*," Jack suggested, "I've got a better idea. Don't."

"Pay ransom," the chief said, holding out one hand, palm up.

"Anything you—" Jean started to say, but Jack clapped a hand over Jean's mouth.

"I don't think so," he said to the chief. "We're not paying to get her back. Frankly, she's not the most pleasant traveling companion. Threw our swabbing mop overboard, she did. You're very welcome to her."

"MMMMMMMMMMMMMMMMPH!" Marcella roared into the ground.

Jean tried to struggle free from Jack, but the captain held him firmly. Jean recognized the look in the chief's eyes. It was the same expression Jack had had when he first met Marcella and realized she would be staying on his ship.

"No ransom?" the chief said, shifting uneasily.

"Am I to understand you don't want her either?" Jack said, pretending to be surprised. "But just think what a lovely wife she'll make you."

The chief turned visibly paler.

"MMMMMMMMMPHMMMMMMMMR-RRRFFFMMMMMMFT!" Marcella bellowed, kicking her feet furiously.

"All right, let's go," Jack said, turning to leave without releasing his hold on Jean. "Just think, it's probably safe to get a new mop now."

"No, wait!" the chief cried. "Please take her back! Please!"

"Oh, I dunno, mate," Jack said. "She really seems to like it here."

"MMMMMMMMFFRRRRMMMMB-BLMMMMMGRRRRRRRRRRFFFFTMM-MMMMMMBTTMMMMMPHT!"

"Please!" the chief said again. "We pay you! Gifts! Anything! Anything to save our ears!"

"Gifts?" Jack said, perking up. "Tell me more."

An hour later, the *Black Pearl* was loaded with fresh food and water, enough to last for weeks. Regretfully, Jack let the islanders untie Marcella and take her aboard as well. On the plus side, she was too angry to speak to him. He hoped that would last a long time.

"Thank you," the chief said to Jack, taking

the pirate's hands between his. "We *all* thank you."

"There's still time to change your minds—" Jack offered. The chief shuddered and backed away.

"Here," he said, pressing something small, cold, and heavy into Jack's hand. "For you. To speed your journey away. And please, please— never come back." He turned and hurried up the beach along with the rest of his tribe.

Jack opened his palm and saw a miniature version of one of the stone heads, carved from dark volcanic rock. Flecks of light seemed to gleam inside the hollow eyes, like something inside was watching him. The rock hummed a little with an unfamiliar energy.

"Splendid," Jack said. "I've always liked, um, eerie little heads."

But to his surprise, the minute he stepped on board with the gift, a brisk wind blew up and filled the sails. The *Black Pearl* shot away from the island as if all the heads on Easter Island were blowing together, hurrying the ship on its way.

Delighted, Jack decided he had earned a rest. He left Catastrophe Shane at the helm with strict instructions to aim for China and retired to his cabin for a long nap.

"*The Day of the Shadow is coming. . . .*"

"Shut up," Jack mumbled, keeping his eyes firmly closed. He was determined not to let anything wake him. Especially not cryptic whispering voices.

Er . . . cryptic whispering voices?

"*The Day of the Shadow is coming. . . .*"

Jack cracked open one eyelid. The cabin was shrouded in darkness. All the shutters were closed, letting in only tiny slivers of moonlight. He was lying on his back on the couch.

And *something* was sitting on his chest.

With a gasp, Jack tried to sit up, but the *something* pressed down heavily, pinning him to the cushions. It leaned closer, a grotesque blob of darkness, until it was breathing smoky air into Jack's ear.

"The Day of the Shadow is coming. When the shadow spreads, our armies will rise . . . and the world shall fall."

"Phew," Jack said. "No offense, mate, but you might want to look into this new concept called dental hygiene."

The shadow beast regarded him silently. It seemed to grow heavier, its weight pressing down on Jack's chest until it felt like he was trapped under a stone fortress, wondering if his chest was about to cave in. Jack's breath came in short gasps, and he tried to push the thing away, but his hands went straight through the creature as if there was nothing there.

"*The Day of the Shadow is coming,*" it hissed again.

"Yeah, I *got* that part," Jack huffed.

"*The shadow will spread . . . and you all will die.*"

"Right, well," Jack said, "must admit I'm less keen on that bit."

"*Hrrrrrraaaaaaaarrrrrrrrrrrrrrrrrrrrrrrrrrr,*" the shadow rumbled ominously. Darkness foamed out from inside it, spreading up and around until it filled the cabin, leaving nothing in Jack's sight but roiling black clouds.

"*The Day of the Shadow . . .*" it whispered one more time.

And then it vanished.

Jack started awake. His heart was pounding and he was drenched, his long dreadlocks sticking to his shoulders and his white shirt soaked with sweat. Worse yet, the energy from the second vial of Shadow Gold was gone. His illness hadn't returned completely, but he could sense the shadows lurking in the corners, as if waiting for his strength to ebb a little more. And then there would be more nightmares . . . more sickness . . . more madness. More of everything Jack hated.

And what was "the Day of the Shadow"? How soon would it come?

He found that he was clutching the little stone head. He lifted it to his lips and whispered: "To Shanghai, as fast as you can, my friend. As fast as you can."

CHAPTER FOUR

When Jack stumbled out to the deck the next morning, he noticed several of his crew members looking at him strangely. He peered strangely back at them, and most of them got nervous and sidled away.

But not Barbossa. The first mate glowered at him from the quarterdeck. The ridiculous blue ostrich plumes on his hat danced in the breeze, and the sun sparkled off his lion's head ring. He looked very disgruntled. Even more disgruntled than he normally looked.

"'Allo, Hector," Jack greeted him cheerfully. "Got up on the wrong side of the hammock this morning, did we?"

"Well," said Barbossa, "I suppose *you* are feeling well-rested."

Given his nightmare, Jack was not feeling well-rested at all, but he was careful not to let that show. "Every good captain deserves a good night's sleep once in a while," he said with a grin, pulling out his spyglass to survey the sea ahead of them. To his surprise, there appeared to be land on the horizon. Already?

"Yesss," Barbossa said. "And I suppose bad captains deserve several nights' sleep, do they?"

Jack squinted at him. "What are you on about?" he asked.

"You've been asleep for four days!" Barbossa shouted. "Or at least hiding in your cabin! No response to all our knocking. What kind of a captain abandons his ship for that long?"

"I didn't *abandon* my ship!" Jack said, ruffled and a little disturbed to find out how long he'd slept. "I was right here—terribly busy—er, making plans, I was. And I left Catastrophe Shane with very clear instructions."

"Oh, right," Barbossa said, casting a glare at the hapless pirate standing by the helm. "One of your best ideas so far. Where *exactly* did you tell him to take us?"

"Shanghai," Jack said uneasily. He glanced over Barbossa's shoulder at the shape of land in the distance. "I guess that's it, eh?"

"Oh, yes," Barbossa said. "That . . . or New Holland."

"New Holland?" Jack said. "Is *Old* Holland anywhere near Shanghai? Maybe he just got confused. Anyway, it could be worse. We could have veered off to Australia."

"You dolt! New Holland *is* Australia!"

They both looked at Catastrophe Shane, who looked up at the sky and tried to pretend he wasn't there.

"Australia?" Jack said, squinting. "Are you sure?"

Barbossa held up a map and a compass. "Oh, I am sure."

"Hmm," Jack said thoughtfully. "Never been there. What's their rum like?"

Barbossa threw the map down on the deck and stormed away.

"Sorry, Captain Jack," Catastrophe Shane mumbled. "I just figured I'd keep aiming at the horizon and China would show up eventually."

"A solid theory," Jack said, beckoning Shane away from the helm. "Why don't you let me have that wheel for a while?"

Shane slipped and stumbled back to the

galley as Jack took the helm and steered the ship north. He wasn't worried. All they had to do was sail on past Australia, wind the ship around a few islands, head through the South China Sea, and doubloons to doughnuts, they'd be in Shanghai in no time.

"Everything all right, Jack?" Billy asked, climbing up to the quarterdeck beside the captain. He studied his old friend carefully, evidently wondering if Jack had completely gone around the bend this time.

"Certainly," Jack said. "Still not sure what Shane's piratical strength is going to be, since it's evidently neither fighting nor navigation. But we'll figure it out sooner or later." He wrinkled his nose. "Must admit he definitely *smells* like a pirate."

"So what is the plan, exactly?" Billy asked. "Sail up to Shanghai and ask Mistress Ching for her vial of gold?"

"Er—why?" Jack asked, furrowing his brow. "You don't think that'll work?"

"You're not that charming, Jack," Billy pointed out.

"Slander and calumny!" Jack protested.

"And Mistress Ching is not easily charmed," Billy continued. "Especially considering that we escaped her ships at the Strait of Magellan, which I'm sure she'll not be tremendously pleased about."

"Details," Jack said, flipping his hands dismissively. "We Pirate Lords are big-picture people, Billy. Not like you pedestrian souls with your childish grievances."

"Right," Billy said. "Never petty or vengeful or selfish, Pirate Lords, nooooo."

"Ahoy! A sail! A sail!" Diego called from the crow's nest (where he was once again hiding from Marcella). He leaned over and pointed north. "A red sail! Coming this way! Fast!"

"Another of Mistress Ching's ships?" Billy guessed as Jack pulled out his spyglass.

The approaching ship did look like the junks they had met on the other side of the Pacific Ocean. But there was a difference—the flag flying from the top mast was not the long, thin, red pennant of Mistress Ching's fleet. Instead, it was black and featured a red skeleton dangling in the center . . . a flag Jack had not seen before.

"I don't think so," Jack said slowly. "No, I think this might be a whole new set of friends." He closed the spyglass with a snap. "To the rigging! Stations! Yardarm! Oh, you know what I mean. Quickly, that way!" He leaped to the helm and steered the ship toward land. With luck, he'd be able to zip around the junk and make it to the shelter of the islands north of Australia.

But luck, on this rare occasion, was not with Captain Jack Sparrow. Within moments he heard an ominous scraping sound from the bottom of the *Pearl*'s hull. He exchanged a worried glance with Billy.

"I'm sure it's nothing," Jack said flippantly.

SCRRRRRRRRRAAAAAAAAAAAAPE.

"Jack, stop the ship!" Billy cried, looking over the side. "We're running onto a coral reef—one of the largest I've ever seen!"

Through the clear, emerald green water, the viciously sharp edges of the coral were all too visible. Fish in all the colors of the rainbow darted in and out of little holes and strange plant life waved and wobbled in the crevices. Jagged outcroppings reached nearly to the water's surface, perilously close to the *Pearl*'s vulnerable wooden underbelly.

Jean and Carolina raced up the deck to the enormous anchor. The only way to stop the ship from crashing into the reef (and probably getting stuck there forever) was to drop anchor immediately. Pirates threw themselves at the heavy cable, shoving the winches and levers that held it in place. With a huge splash, the anchor fell to the water and sank rapidly, crashing straight through the intricate lace of the coral reef as it went.

The *Black Pearl* jerked to a halt, pulling the ship around suddenly.

There was a thud from below decks. "OUCH!" Marcella's voice shrieked. "Who threw me out of my hammock? I *hate* you!"

"Brilliant," Jack said. Disaster averted. Well, one disaster, anyway. The other was bearing down on them at top speed, and now it was too late to run. They had no choice but to demand Parlay.

Jack strode to the railing as the strange ship drew closer. The curious yellow eyes painted on the sides of the junk seemed to be staring at him, reading his soul and seeing his nightmares. The sails looked like dragon wings, curved and strengthened with bamboo supports. They flicked and quivered in the wind, adjusting to every change in the breeze. Jack could also see that the bottom of the ship was flat, so it rode higher in the water than the Pearl, making it easier for the strange ship to skim over the top of the coral reef.

The hull of the new ship was painted in bright, garish colors such as green and orange, making a striking contrast to the sleek black *Pearl*. It skimmed up alongside and dropped anchor only a few feet away from where Jack was standing. Jack tried to look unconcerned, as if he had planned this meeting all along and was just hanging out on this coral reef waiting for an enemy ship to come by.

Asian faces watched him closely and silently from the other ship, all the pirates standing at attention with their hands clasped behind their backs.

"Good morning," Jack called across. "Fine weather we're having."

They stared at him in stony stillness.

"Tell me, is this the way to Shanghai?" Jack asked them. "We thought we'd take a shortcut—not sure it's working out for us."

No reaction; nothing but blank expressions.

"Huh," Jack remarked. "Maybe they're under a curse. Wonder if we can get one of those for Marcella."

"Or maybe they actually respect their captain," Barbossa muttered, nodding to the man who was striding out of the captain's quarters on the other ship.

The captain was strikingly tall and fierce-looking. His head was shaved completely bald, with only a long, dark beard and moustache framing his mouth. A small scar marred his face below his right eye, but otherwise he had handsome, strong features. Jack guessed that he was not Chinese, but instead came from somewhere in South Asia—perhaps Siam or Singapore.

Jade stones, ranging in color from a dark jungle green to a pale, marbled white-green, decorated his armor-plated belt, rings, shoulder guard, and wristbands. His dark green robes were lined with red silk and embroidered with dragons in golden thread. A long sword hung in a black, lacquered wood scabbard from his belt, opposite a wicked-looking pistol.

The captain studied the crew of the *Black Pearl* for a long moment. Finally a small smile crossed his face.

"What a most fortunate meeting this is," he said in polished, accented English, inclining his head toward them. "The gods have indeed given us their favor today." His hand swept out, indicating his ship. A gold ring on his hand gleamed in the sunlight. "Please, come aboard the *Empress* so we can meet properly." His smile deepened, becoming more menacing, and a spark of shrewd calculation flickered in his deep, dark eyes.

"Oh, that's all right," Jack said. "Quite happy over here, thanks."

"No, really," the man said. "I insist." His men subtly shifted, placing their hands on their weapons.

"And who is doing the inviting, if I might ask?" Jack inquired.

The captain's sly expression hinted at the reaction he expected to get. "Me?" he said. "Is it not obvious? I am Sao Feng."

CHAPTER FIVE

"**S**ao Feng, Sao Feng," Jack repeated, turning over the name. He shook his head. "Nope, never heard of 'im."

Now the captain frowned, the kind of frown that would make most men quake in their boots. "Never heard of me!" he barked. "I'm only the fiercest captain to ever sail the South China Sea! The Seven Seas, in fact!"

"The fiercest, eh? Then shouldn't you be the

Pirate Lord of Singapore and the South China Sea?" Jack asked, deliberately needling him. "Last I heard, it was a fellow by the name of Liang Dao."

Sao Feng's face darkened even further. His hand gripped the hilt of his sword. "Liang Dao is my older brother," he snarled. "He inherited the title of Pirate Lord from our father." From his emphasis on the word "inherited," it was fairly clear what Sao Feng thought of Liang Dao's fitness for the role.

"Ah. That's sort of how *you* became a Pirate Lord, isn't it, Jack?" Barbossa said snidely.

"Not exactly," Jack said, shooting his first mate a stern look. "Well, it's complicated."

Sao Feng blinked, eyeing Jack closely. "You?" he said. "You—a Pirate Lord? Ha!"

Jack swept his hat into a flamboyant bow. "Captain Jack Sparrow, Pirate Lord of the Caribbean," he announced. "Has a nice ring to it, doesn't it? Sticks in your head. Sounds rakish and majestic all at once, like a proper pirate captain. Not at all silly-sounding like, say, hypothetically, off the top of my head, Smarbossa."

Barbossa scowled.

The captain of the *Empress* looked meaningfully at the Pacific Ocean, sparkling brightly all around them. "Rather far from home, aren't you, Captain Sparrow?"

"Are we? I hadn't noticed," Jack answered. He too looked around at the blue-green water, making a puzzled face as if it had snuck up on him.

Sao Feng snorted impatiently. "What are you doing here?" He touched the hilt of his sword warningly. "And do not even think about telling me anything other than the absolute truth."

"Seeing the world, mate," Jack said, flinging his arms open. "Enjoying the freedom of the open sea. Any laws against that?"

"We are also looking for the Pirate Lords who hold the vials of Shadow Gold," said a monotone voice behind Jack, "so that we can defeat the Shadow Lord."

Jack whirled around, outraged. Zombie Alex stared blankly at him. Jack's eyes widened and his nose arched into a vicious, disgusted scowl.

"Well, fine," Jack said. "Why don't you just tell the strange man all our secrets, then?" Alex obeyed, opening his mouth. Jack added hurriedly, "No, don't say anything! Don't speak again until he's gone!"

Alex obediently shut up, but it was too late.

"Shadow Gold?" Sao Feng echoed. "That sounds . . . valuable."

"Oh, it's nothing," Jack said, waving the topic aside. "You wouldn't like it, trust me. Nasty stuff. Although—I don't suppose you've seen any, have you?"

Sao Feng narrowed his eyes and didn't reply.

"No?" Jack tried. "Your brother hasn't recently come into possession of a lovely little vial of really very unimportant, hardly worth mentioning, liquidy shiny stuff?"

"Ah," Sao Feng said, his face a perfect mask. "Perhaps I know of what you speak."

"Really?" Jack perked up. "Then maybe we do have something to discuss."

"As I said before"—Sao Feng bowed slightly and lifted one elegant hand toward his quarters at the rear of the junk—"I insist."

"This doesn't seem like a wise idea," Billy said in a low voice to Jack. "I don't think we can trust him."

"Well, of course we can't," Jack retorted. "I mean, he is a *pirate*, after all. I rather think he can't trust us, either." Shaking his head as if he thought Billy was quite daft, Jack vaulted to the top of the wooden railing, seized a trailing rope, and swung himself across to the *Empress*.

On board the other ship, a skinny man with a sparse moustache, wearing a long leather cloak, stepped forward as if to stand between Jack and Sao Feng. Sao Feng waved him off.

"Do not fear, Tai Huang," the *Empress's* captain said. "I am sure our new friend will not do anything . . . foolish."

"Foolish? Me?" Jack said. "Never!" He grinned so his gold tooth sparkled in the bright sun.

Carolina leaped to the rail of the *Pearl* and swung across after Jack. She landed lightly on the deck of the *Empress* and immediately found herself surrounded by a bristling thicket of swords.

"I'm not leaving my *capitán* alone over here!" she said bravely, reaching for her own sword.

"Stand down, stand down," Sao Feng said to

his crew. "I admire a woman with courage, especially one with such grace," he said to her gallantly.

Sao Feng took Carolina's hand and bowed to kiss it. Carolina tossed back her ebony hair, looking every inch the princess she was, despite her disheveled pirate garb and bare feet.

"I believe the Pirate Code allows the captain to bring a few members of his crew to Parlay, doesn't it?" she said, arching her eyebrows.

"Someone has been studying their *Pirata Codex*," Sao Feng said smoothly. "You are correct. Does anyone else wish to join his . . . or her . . . captain on my ship?"

Most of the pirates on the *Pearl* shuffled their feet and gazed at the sky.

"Barbossa will join us," Jack said, flicking his fingers easily to beckon Barbossa across. "Come along, Hector."

Glowering balefully, Jack's first mate joined

Jack and Carolina on board the Empress. With a regal nod, Sao Feng escorted the three of them over to his quarters.

Jack managed not to gasp in astonishment as he stepped down the elegantly carved wooden staircase into Sao Feng's cabin, but it was difficult. His own cabin did not begin to compare to Sao Feng's quarters. This struck Jack as very unfair.

The room was opulent and richly decorated with swaths of fine silks, priceless jade carvings, bronze incense burners, antique vases, and elaborately woven tapestries. Soft pillows and layers of Oriental rugs covered part of the floor and candlelight glowed from the lanterns, mingling with incense smoke to create a warm, luxurious den, untouched by the bright sunlight outside. Sao Feng was obviously a man who liked his luxuries—and also dark, underground spaces.

Two figures rose from the pillows as they entered.

"Speaking of luxuries . . ." Jack muttered to himself, his eyes widening.

Standing before them were two strikingly beautiful Asian women; Jack guessed they might be twins. Each wore long, dark red silk robes with a bright red sash at the waist. Golden dragons wound sensuously around the curves of the robes, embroidered in fine silk thread. A glint of steel in their dark hair revealed the chopsticks holding their elaborate coiffures in place.

Jack winked at the one closest to him. She immediately whipped out a silk fan to hide her face, but not before Jack caught a glimmer of a smile.

"These are my attendants," Sao Feng said. He was busy at a low table, so he missed the flirtatious glances Jack was exchanging with the two women. "Lian and Park."

"Attendants?" Carolina asked. "Are they pirates? Female pirates?" She couldn't keep the excitement out of her voice.

"Everyone on this ship is a pirate," Sao Feng said gravely. "And my fair companions are two of the most deadly."

Carolina looked doubtfully at Lian, who closed her fan with a snap and then flipped it open with a sharp motion that made Carolina realize that the edge of the fan was razor sharp—and that the woman wielding it could easily slice someone's throat open with it.

"I wouldn't mind being killed by one of those," Jack whispered to Barbossa, who rolled his eyes in disgust. Jack wiggled his fingers at Park and then hid his grin quickly as Sao Feng turned around with a pale porcelain teapot in his hand.

"Please join me," Sao Feng said, indicating the pillows around the table. "We have business to discuss."

Jack, Barbossa, and Carolina knelt around the table. Jack made sure to position himself so he was facing Lian and Park, who had moved over to the far wall and were now studying him with half their faces hidden behind their fans. He was sure he heard one of them giggle quietly.

Sao Feng poured tea from the pot into delicate china cups, handing one to each of his visitors. Carolina leaned over to let the strong herbal-smelling steam waft across her face. Jack sniffed it suspiciously.

"Hmm. Tea. Don't suppose you have any rum, do you?" he asked Sao Feng.

"Certainly not. Believe me, you will not want to be under its influence for the rest of our conversation," the captain said.

"Oh, I rather think I will," Jack said dolefully.

"Let's get on with it," Barbossa interrupted. "I take it there's something you want from us, isn't there?" He gave Sao Feng a challenging look.

Sao Feng held his cup between his long fingers and sipped his tea. Finally his intelligent, calculating gaze settled on the *Black Pearl's* first mate.

"I believe what we have here is an opportunity," he said. "An opportunity to make a bargain for mutual benefit." He blinked, and Carolina got the feeling that "mutual" was always a bit of an exaggeration when it came to Sao Feng.

"Right," Jack said. "You tell us where the Shadow Gold is, and we go on our merry way and leave you alone. Sounds mutually beneficial to me."

"I am looking for something," Sao Feng continued as if Jack hadn't spoken. "My brother Liang Dao, the current Pirate Lord of Singapore, has sent me on this voyage so far south to find an object of great value . . . the Deep Sea Opal."

"I like the sound of that," Jack said, a smile spreading across his face.

"It is a legendary black opal," Sao Feng said softly, "as big as a man's fist and shimmering with hidden fire. Legend says that any man who possesses it will earn great fortune, power, and fame."

"Come again?" Now Jack was even more interested. "Did you say 'fortune'?"

"However," Sao Feng went on, "there is one small problem. The opal's power will not go to anyone who steals it. Only those who receive the opal as a gift will benefit from its glorious effects; the man who is foolhardy enough to steal the opal will be cursed forever."

Jack glanced at Lian and Park uneasily. He didn't like where this was going.

"Hsst," Park hissed suddenly, flicking her fan closed and then open again. "Liang Dao is a coward!"

"He wouldn't dare come for the opal himself," Lian agreed, her dark eyes flashing. "He wants brave Sao Feng to steal it for him, so Liang Dao can have all of the power and none of the curse!"

"I see," Jack said thoughtfully.

"He fears you," Park said to Sao Feng. "He knows you would be the greatest Pirate Lord the world had ever seen."

"You might not know this, love," Jack said, "but I'm actually a Pirate Lord, too." She tilted her head at him, and he added, "So, you know, second greatest, maybe."

"My brother is a fool in many ways," Sao Feng said, "but for once he has arrived at a clever plan. I am not the kind of man who is afraid of hobgoblins and fairy tales. I do not entirely believe there is any power in this opal beyond the value it will hold as a precious gem. But the pirates who serve under us would never follow a man who had stolen the Deep Sea Opal. So despite the fact that I do not fear any sort of curse, I cannot steal it."

"The men would believe he was cursed with bad luck for the rest of his days," Lian said in a hushed whisper.

"He is trying to crush your ambition," Park said, making a fist with one hand. "But it won't work! We won't let it!"

"We don't have to," Sao Feng said with a sly smile. He stared straight at Jack. "We have a perfect solution right in front of us."

Jack twisted around to look behind him, then searched theatrically all around him, peering under the low table and lifting his hands in bewilderment. "No solution here, mate."

"Captain Jack Sparrow," Sao Feng said in a voice of steel. "*You* will steal the Deep Sea Opal for me."

CHAPTER SIX

"**O**h, you've got the wrong fellow," Jack said. "Jack Sparrow doesn't *steal* things. I *liberate* them. Mostly they just appear in my hands. Quite mysterious, really."

"Like the jade dragon you slipped up your sleeve earlier?" Sao Feng said darkly.

Jack tried to look innocent for a moment, but now Barbossa was glaring at him, too. Finally Jack shook his arm and a small jade carving bounced out of the end of his sleeve. He feigned astonishment. "See what I mean? How did that get there?"

"Oh, *Jack*," Carolina said in a disappointed voice.

"Oh, *Captain* Jack," Jack reminded her.

"You will steal the opal and give it to me," Sao Feng said. "And then I shall have its power instead of Liang Dao."

"And what do we get out of it?" Jack demanded.

"We don't want to sail with a cursed *capitán* either!" Carolina exclaimed.

"Who would?" Barbossa agreed. "Really, it's a sign of a poor captain if he can't avoid curses."

"You want the Shadow Gold," Sao Feng said. "I want the Deep Sea Opal." He crossed his arms and leaned back against green silk pillows. "You decide."

Jack wound his fingers in his beard, thinking hard. Was there a way around this? Surely there had to be. Wouldn't it be lovely if he could get that opal for himself? But more important, he needed the Shadow Gold. After the nightmares, he needed it more urgently than ever. He couldn't afford to sink into any more four-day slumbers. And he never wanted to smell that smoky breath in his face again. Perhaps the legends of the opal were only that—legends. Maybe it was all a hoax and nothing terrible would happen. Of course, given Jack's prior experience with horrible supernatural thingies, he had a feeling it was all too real. But he had no choice.

"All right." Jack sighed. "Where's this opal, then?"

Sao Feng pointed down at the floorboards. Identical smiles crossed the faces of his attendants.

"Er—south?" Jack guessed. "Right . . . New Zealand, maybe?"

Barbossa rolled his eyes.

"Where would you expect the Deep Sea Opal to be, Jack Sparrow?" Sao Feng asked drily.

"Sitting on a nice island somewhere?" Jack guessed desperately. "Out in the open, like, where anyone can stroll up and take it?"

"Deep, deep under the sea," Sao Feng said deliberately. "Down in the watery depths."

"Oh, no," said Jack. "No, no, no. I don't deal with mermaids anymore, mate. No stealing from them, no making deals with them, none of that. I learned my lesson a long time ago. Actually, it's a funny story, if you want to hear it—"

"I know of no mermaids," Sao Feng interrupted him. "The spirits are different here. The one who guards the Deep Sea Opal is known as the Rainbow Serpent."

That didn't sound much better than mermaids to Jack, quite frankly.

"But whether you speak of merfolk or

rainbow serpents it should be no matter," Sao Feng continued. "These are just things of folklore meant to scare away those who might steal the gem. You will encounter neither beast nor finned woman, I assure you. Lian will accompany you. To ensure there are no tricks."

"Tricks!" Jack said, pressing his hand to his chest like he was mortally offended. "As if I would ever—well, no, that seems fair, actually." Behind Sao Feng's back, he blew Lian a kiss. She hid her face behind the fan again, then peeked out at him with a flirtatious sparkle in her eyes.

"Well, I am not going," Barbossa said, putting his foot down. "Yer not getting me to the bottom of the ocean, I don't care what ye say."

"Fine. I'll take Diego and Billy with me. Your big, stupid hat would probably keep you from sinking down to the depths anyway," Jack said.

Carolina frowned at him. She knew Jack well enough by now to know that he was hoping to trick his friends into stealing the opal for him.

But if that was his plan, it wasn't going to work. Back out in the sunshine, Carolina managed to take Diego aside to warn him before the group set off.

"Be careful, Diego," she said, squeezing his hands. "Don't touch that opal. Don't go anywhere near it. And don't let Captain Jack talk you into taking it, because he can be very clever that way."

"Stop worrying," Diego said, brushing her hair out of her face lightly. "It'll be all right."

"Oh, *Diego*!" Marcella cried, knocking Carolina to the ground and flinging her arms around Diego's neck. "I'm so *frightened* for you! You're so brave!" She stepped back and flapped her eyelashes at him. "Listen, if you see anything else down there that this Rainbow Serpent can spare—any smaller opals or pearls or pretty jewelry of any kind—well, I would be *so* charmed if you'd bring something back for me, dear, sweet Diego. I mean, it *is* my birthday . . . in a couple of months."

Carolina climbed to her feet again, amused at the mix of terror and confusion on Diego's face.

"Come on, Diego, lad!" Jack called, waving him over to the railing of the *Pearl*. "No time like the present for deep-sea diving and confronting serpents and liberating mystical opals, I always say."

Sao Feng stood at the rail of the *Empress*, watching closely as Jack removed his beloved hat and entrusted it to Carolina's care. After some thought, Jack also removed his boots and set them carefully beside the railing. He rolled up the sleeves of his white linen shirt, revealing a blue sparrow tattoo on his right arm. Sao Feng raised his eyebrows at the *P* that was branded on Jack's wrist just below the sparrow.

"You have encountered the East India Trading Company, I see," he said.

"Oh, it's nothing," Jack said, waving his hand in the air. "Small misunderstanding. Are they over here, too? They really ought to think about changing their name to Whole Flaming Planet Trading Company, shouldn't they?"

"Ready, Jack?" Billy said from beside him.

Lian stepped up to Jack's side. He beamed at her. "'Allo, love," he said. "Stay close to me; I'll take care of you."

"Yes," she said, leaning in seductively, "I think we *should* stay close." Jack realized that while he'd been staring into her eyes, she had been tying their wrists together with a firmly knotted silk scarf. He tugged on it, but there was no escaping now.

"Right," he said. "Well, if that's the way you like it, darling—"

Before he could finish his sentence, Lian

yanked him up onto the railing, and then dove into the crystal blue sea. With a yelp, Jack was dragged along behind her.

He managed to inhale a deep breath before they sank below the surface. Lian began kicking her feet immediately, scissoring swiftly through the waves, swimming deeper and deeper. Jack saw Diego and Billy splash into the water above them. Soon they were all diving down into the ocean depths.

They swam past intricate castles of coral inhabited by schools of sunshine yellow fish, translucent pink jelly man o' wars, and placid sea turtles that watched them swim by with bewildered expressions. Waving fronds of sea-weed brushed their feet and sleek dolphins darted around them, inviting them to play. Explosions of bubbles burst like fireworks as clumps of fish suddenly darted out of their way. The water was so clear that Jack could see for miles across the coral reef, and down almost to the ocean floor. It was one of the most beautiful places he had ever been, and he imagined he would quite enjoy it if he weren't tied to a pirate and on his way to pick up a new curse.

Well, maybe he wouldn't even mind the "being tied to a pirate" part, considering how attractive this particular pirate was.

But she was also determined, and possibly able to breathe underwater, since she was still swimming at the same pace while Jack's lungs felt like they were about to burst. Down, down, down they went, beyond the reach of the sun, into the mysterious, dark ocean depths. Jack was beginning to see stars. He tried to pull at the scarf with his free hand, but there was no chance of getting it loose. Lian glanced around at him, her long, dark hair swirling around her in the water.

She pointed at a cave up ahead. He pointed at

his mouth, then up at the surface. She shook her head and kept swimming. He really wished he could make a smart remark right about now.

Suddenly the cave was right in front of them, and as they swam into it, as if crossing an invisible barrier, they fell to the sandy floor in an airy cavern. Jack sprawled onto his back, gasping for breath. Even Lian was panting a little. She leaned over him, gazing into his eyes.

"Listen, love," Jack said. "Normally I like to get to know a girl before I let her tie me up and nearly drown me. But in your case, I'll make an exception." She ducked away from him quickly, revealing that she had untied the sash that was holding their wrists together. He stretched out his arm, relishing the feeling of freedom.

Billy and Diego crashed into the cave, rolling to a stop beside Jack in a flurry of sand.

"*Madre de Dios!* There's air down here!" Diego cried, jumping to his feet and looking around. "What kind of witchcraft is this?"

"Why, haven't you been in an enchanted, mystical, underwater cavern before?" Jack asked. "They're everywhere, apparently. Really nothing to get excited about."

Jack was hiding a sense of uneasiness from his friends. He had actually been in a cavern very similar to this more than once, when he was a teenager and captain of the *Barnacle*. In order to save his friends from the sirens' song, he'd swum down to a cave like this to bargain with some very disagreeable mermaids. And he'd nearly wound up being trapped there as their prisoner for life, too. He shuddered. He couldn't bear to think about it. Billy had heard the story during his and Jack's earliest adventures, and he and Jack had been trapped by the merfolk more than once.*

---

* Jack's adventures under *Isla Sirena* are chronicled in Jack Sparrow Vols. 2, *The Siren Song*; 4, *The Sword of Cortés*; 11, *Poseidon's Peak*; and 12, *Bold New Horizons*.

Luckily, however, those mermaids were on the other side of the world, in the Caribbean. Hopefully there wouldn't be any Scaly Tails, as Jack called them, in *this* cave. The turquoise light reflecting off the coral reef walls was similar to the mermaids' cave, but here the coral that spiraled all around them was pink and white instead of black, creating a much lighter, friendlier atmosphere. That suited Jack just fine.

A tunnel led off from the back of the cave, with a glowing multicolored light at the end of it. Tiny rainbows shimmered in the nooks and crannies of the coral reef as the pirates tiptoed cautiously along the tunnel. Jack nimbly jumped over the pools of turquoise water on the floor. He admired how lightly and gracefully Lian slipped along beside him. She smiled when she saw him watching her.

Suddenly the tunnel opened out into an enormous cave. Lian grabbed Jack's arm and pulled him backward behind a coral outcropping. Billy and Diego crouched behind them. They all stared out at the source of the rainbow light.

A giant snake filled the entire cavern. Jack couldn't imagine how it got in and out—it seemed far too large to fit through the tunnel where he and his friends were crouching. Perhaps it never left. To be trapped in a cave forever, cut off from the sounds of the waves and the smell of the fresh sea air and the bracing wind of freedom . . . that sounded like Jack's worst nightmare.

Sunrise-bright clouds and swirling colors that Jack had never seen before shifted through the serpent's iridescent scales. The tip of its tail, gleaming lavender-indigo–midnight blue, rested near where they were hiding, and the serpent's coils took up almost every inch of floor space.

Diego pointed over Jack's shoulder to the serpent's head, where forest green scales seemed to overlap with seashell pink and pale ivory, then changed as they watched to fiery reds and oranges. Its eyes were closed, and its long forked tongue flicked in and out as it slept.

But more interesting still was what was just *beyond* the serpent's head: another cave. It was the only other exit from this room. And based on the serpent's position, it was clearly guarding whatever was inside that cave.

Jack signaled to the others for silence. Slowly and carefully, in tense quiet, the four pirates slid around the serpent's tail and tiptoed across the cave. They held their breath as they squeezed past, making sure to not even brush against the snake's shimmering scales. It was a delicate dance, finding the next safe place to set a foot down.

But finally they made it across to the far wall and darted past the snake's tongue. One by one, they ducked into the last cave.

In the center was a pool of clear water, lit by a glow from within. As they drew closer, they could see something shining from the center of the pool. It was an enormous black stone, shimmering with colors and gleaming with a mysterious inner light.

They had found the Deep Sea Opal.

CHAPTER SEVEN

The four pirates stood around the pool for a moment, staring at their prize—so close, and yet so cursed.

"I say, Diego," Jack whispered finally, "could you just reach in and grab that for me? I don't want to get my hands wet." He lifted his hands in the air—not his cleverest trick, as he was still drenched from head to toe after the swim down through the ocean.

"No, senor!" Diego said. "*You* grab it! This is your quest."

"Whatever happened to all your respect for your captain?" Jack wanted to know. He made a grievously wounded face. "What happened to being a loyal crew member, Diego?"

"I *am* loyal," Diego said, "but with the whole Spanish navy after Carolina and me, I need all the luck I can get. I can't afford to make it worse. *Lo siento*—I'm sorry, Jack."

"All right," Jack said. "Billy? How's about it? Do an old chum a favor?"

"Don't even try," Billy said darkly. "This was your idea, Jack."

Jack sighed deeply. There *had* to be a way to get the opal without cursing himself. He glanced hopefully at Lian, but he could see from her sly smile that he'd have no luck there.

He edged closer to the pool, mesmerized by

the glimmering rock at its center. It wouldn't be hard to reach into the water . . . with just one movement, it could be his . . . but what if the curse was real? He couldn't afford another curse. Not with creepy little shadow beasties already haunting him.

Suddenly, the surface of the pool began to bubble. Jack jumped back.

"What's it doing?" he asked. "Why is it doing that?"

Tiny bubbles foamed to the surface, faster and faster until the opal was hidden beneath the spray. Jack felt a moment of panic as the opal vanished. What if someone else was stealing it right now? He lunged forward to plunge his arm into the pool, but just as his fingers touched the water, a shape rose through the bubbles and burst into the air in front of him.

With a shout, Jack fell back against the coral. He rubbed his eyes, blinked several times, and then rubbed them again. Billy and Diego were staring openmouthed at the pool. Or, rather, at the pool's new inhabitant.

"Oh, bloody hell," Jack said. "I believe I was promised no mermaids."

"Did you misssss usssss, Jack Sssparrow?" the mermaid asked, narrowing her haunting dark eyes at him. She pulled herself out to sit on a rock, and the others gasped, seeing her bright blue tail for the first time.

"I wouldn't say I *missed* you, precisely," Jack said to the familiar Scaly Tail. "More like I hoped never to see you again, to be honest."

"Honesssst?" the mermaid sniffed. "You? You who cheated usssss out of your eternal companionship?"

"I *am* good company," Jack agreed, "so I can see why you'd hold a grudge about that. Still, it's been quite a long time, you know."

"Our kind never forget," she said. "And

you've brought friends along. Thisssss one I know," she said, motioning to Billy, "but the othersssss . . ."

"Oh, these folks. Yes, right. Diego, Lian—meet Morveren. Morveren, Diego, and Lian. Okay. Done? Good. And now how about you? Where're your friends? Don't think I've ever seen you without Aquala and Aqueduct or whatever she's called."

"Aquila," Morveren corrected. "They are otherwise occupied."

"Yes, you have seemed to have a lot of trouble in merfolkland since I liberated your subjects all those years ago, haven't you?"*

Morveren hissed.

"What's that? Bitterness? Rather undeserved, I'd say," Jack said. "You were the ones who tried

---

* Jack freed the merfolk of the Blue-tails' (Morveren and her sisters') rule in *Jack Sparrow* Vol. 12, *Bold New Horizons*.

to trick me out of my freedom the first time we met."*

Morveren spread her hands to suggest that he should expect that kind of thing from her. "Mermaid," she said.

Jack made the same gesture. "Pirate!" he said.

"Hmm," she said. "Touché."

"What is she doing here now?" Diego asked Jack.

"I might ask you the ssssame quessssssstion," Morveren said. "Why are you here, Jack Ssssparrow? Looking for ssssssomething?"

"No, no," Jack said blithely. "Just passing through. Isn't this the way to Shanghai? Don't tell me we're lost again. I blame Barbossa."

Morveren stared at him with cold eyes. She lifted one hand and clicked her webbed fingers. Suddenly the light in the room went dim. The

* *Jack Sparrow* Vol. 2, *The Siren Song.*

pirates turned to find the Rainbow Serpent's head blocking the entrance to the cave. And now the snake was quite awake, much more awake than Jack really liked his beasties to be. It blinked enormous orange eyes at them and its tongue flickered within inches of where they stood.

"All right," Jack said, throwing caution to the wind. "Here's the truth. We've come to get that opal, but we don't want to steal it, because of the curse. Not saying we won't, just saying—we're open to other options. Why steal when you can negotiate, eh?"

The mermaid tilted her head at him. "How refreshingly honesssst of you, Jack Sssssparrow."

"I'm like that sometimes," Jack said. "More often than you'd think. Always catches people off guard, though."

Morveren said something in a hissing, clicking language to the snake. It hissed back at her.

"The Rainbow Sssssserpent says a trade might be acceptable to him," Morveren said, "if you have anything of equal value." Her blue tail flicked against the rock.

"Oh, no," Jack said. "I'm not falling for that trick. No one will ever steal my freedom from me again!" He paused to think for a moment. "Would you like one of them instead?" he asked, pointing to Diego and Billy.

"Jack!" Billy protested.

"*Captain* Jack!" Jack responded in the same outraged tone. "Oh, all right, you can't have them either."

"The Sssssserpent is more agreeable than I am," Morveren said. "He will accept an alternative. What do you have to offer?"

Jack thought. He felt through the trinkets woven into his braids. Each represented a different adventure. He had already added a tiny silver llama to symbolize his meeting with the

113

Incas. But nothing he could find in his hair seemed worthy of trade for the opal. "Too bad," he said, thinking of the knotted string *quipu* Tia Dalma had given him.* "I had this lovely kee-poo you might have liked. If you're into knotted string, that is." He was glad he had left his hat on the *Pearl*—imagine if the serpent had demanded that! Jack would never give up his marvelous hat!

Billy and Diego were searching their pockets, so Jack did the same. A couple of doubloons, a few crumbs of hardtack, and a pair of loaded dice rolled through his hands. Then his fingers touched something cold and heavy.

He pulled it out and discovered the tiny stone head they'd been given on Rapa Nui.

He also distinctly saw Morveren's eyes light up when she saw it.

---

* In Vol. 1, *The Caribbean.*

"Well, there's this," he said, slowly turning it between his fingers. "But it's *so* valuable . . . I really don't know if I can bear to part with it. Tell you what—"

"No," Morveren said quickly.

"You don't know what I was going to say!" Jack objected.

"You were going to propose a duel," Morveren said.

"All right," Jack admitted. "You did know what I was going to say."

"A duel like the one you used to sssslither out of our deal last time," Morveren said.

"Oh, yes," Jack said, "it was definitely *me* doing the 'sssssslithering,' what with you making me fight lots of giant toothy beasties. Certainly *I* was the tricky one there!"

"We will not accept a duel thisssss time," Morveren said, folding her arms and setting her jaw stubbornly. "A trade or nothing. You give us that sssssstone head, and we'll give you the opal. Else, you leave with nothing. And 'nothing' includes your lives. 'Ssssavvy?'"

That sounded more than fair to Jack, but he knew he had to make Morveren think she had gotten the better end of the bargain. "Ooooooohhhh," he said as if the idea pained him. "I don't *know* . . . it's such a *precious* little head . . . I mean, we use it *allllll* the time."

"Yeah," Diego said, catching on. "You can't let go of that, Jack! It would be a terrible loss! Just crushing!"

"It is that or nothing!" Morveren thundered. "You have two choicesssss: accept the trade, or be eaten by the Rainbow Sssssserpent!"

Sssssssssssssssssssssssssssssssssssssss, agreed the snake.

"Well, when you put it that way," said Jack. He sighed theatrically. "I suppose we have no choice." He held out the stone head, shaking his head as if he were about to cry.

Morveren reached into the water and picked up the opal. It gleamed with hidden fire as she lifted it into the air. Jack stepped up to her, and in one motion, they traded objects.

Jack hid his glee. The opal was his, fair and square. He hadn't stolen it, so he wouldn't be cursed!

"Now get out," Morveren said. "And don't come down to thissssss area of the seasssss again, Jack Sparrow. "

"Not frightening me," Jack said.

Morveren glared at him.

Diego tugged on his sleeve. "Come on, Jack, before you really say something stupid."

"By your leave," Jack said, bowing deeply to the mermaid and the serpent. The four of them edged out past the snake's gleaming scales, hurried across the floor, and ducked into the tunnel. As they ran toward the cave mouth at the end of the tunnel, Jack grinned sideways at Billy.

"Admit it, Bill," he said, "you love this."

Billy snorted. "Yes. Nearly being eaten by serpents is my idea of fun." Billy jumped through the barrier and started swimming away, with Diego close behind him.

Jack turned to Lian and held out his wrist. "Ready to be tied up again, love?"

She giggled, shaking her head, and then ran forward and dove across the barrier.

Just beyond the barrier was the roaring sound of spinning water that was all too familiar to Jack and Billy. A waterspout portal. Lian had jumped in and had probably been sucked up to the surface already.

Jack carefully wrapped the opal in his vest. "This part's fun," he said to Diego.

Billy raised an eyebrow. He'd been severely injured in the merfolk's waterspout portals before.

The portal spun like a funnel in the water

before them. Jack motioned to Billy and Diego to follow him, then he jumped into the portal. The whirling water spun so fast that Jack couldn't understand which way was up. Fish, seaweed, shattered shells, flotsam, and jetsam spun around him in the water. And then he was bobbing on the surface. Right behind him, Billy and Diego shot up out of the water.

But as soon as the three of them had broken the surface, something tugged at Jack's braids. For a moment he thought it was just the water—but when he glanced sideways, he saw two shadows darting on either side of him like demonic fish. They wove through his hair, pulling him back under. One floated in front of his face for a moment, then shot up his nose. Immediately he felt like he couldn't breathe. The anchors in his chest were back, dragging him farther away from the surface, down into death. The shadow illness had chosen the perfect moment to try to kill him.

Jack flailed his arms and legs, kicking and fighting with desperate strength. He could feel the energy draining out of his whole body. The spooky darkness of the ocean depths seemed closer than the light up above. He was *not* going to drown. He *refused* to drown. What an ignominious death for a pirate. Captain Jack Sparrow, greatest pirate in the world, was not going to die this way.

CHAPTER EIGHT

Just as Jack thought he was about to lose consciousness, a grip of steel locked around his wrist and yanked him upwards. Lian's robes swirled around him as she towed him to the surface. She'd returned for him! Jack snorted out a spray of bubbles and saw one of the shadows go spinning away.

Lian and Jack burst into the open air. Jack inhaled deeply, filling his lungs until his heart was calm again.

"Are you all right?" Lian asked anxiously.

"See, I knew you liked me," Jack said with a wink. "Just wanted you to prove it."

"Do you have it?" Sao Feng called eagerly from above them. "Do you have the opal?" He leaned over the railing of the *Pearl*, the sun reflecting off the dome of his head. Apparently while they had been gone, Sao Feng had moved ships. Jack's crew lined the rail, peering down at him curiously. Jack noticed that Carolina was even more delighted to see Diego than Marcella was. (Marcella was too busy throwing a tantrum over the fact that Diego had brought her no precious jewels from the treasure trove she imagined at the bottom of the ocean.) Perhaps Carolina was finally starting to notice the lad after all.

Billy and Diego hurried up the rope ladder to the deck, followed by Lian, and then Jack. Jack took his hat from Carolina's outstretched arms and clapped it on top of his wet head, instantly feeling much better. A good hat made all the difference.

"Well?" Sao Feng demanded.

"First I want to know about the vial," Jack said cagily. "You said you would tell me where it is."

"Did I?" Sao Feng said. "I believe if you think carefully, the terms are not quite so clear. I implied I would help you find it. But to do that, you will have to accompany me back to Singapore."

"Go with you!" said Jack. "That's not exactly my style, mate. I'm not much of a follower."

"Not much of a leader, either," Barbossa muttered, but only Diego heard him. The Spanish sailor filed that away in his mind with the other suspicious comments he'd heard from the first mate.

"Besides, it's not very subtle, showing up with

an entourage," Jack said with a grimace. "It's rather flashy. Hallo, over here, come to steal your Shadow Gold, ta very much. Savvy?"

"Trust me," Sao Feng said in a manner that did not inspire trust at all. "This is the best way for you to get your Shadow Gold. You need my help." He held out his hand. "Now. The opal."

Jack touched the smooth surface of the stone tucked inside his vest. The temptation of all that power was very strong . . . but the memory of the shadows trying to drown him was stronger. Resigned, he pulled out the opal and plopped it into Sao Feng's hand.

"Beautiful," Sao Feng whispered, holding up the opal to watch it sparkle in the sunlight. "Just as I dreamed." He formed a thin-lipped smile. "Liang Dao will be so pleased."

The busy, dilapidated streets and stinking markets of Singapore were infested with agents of the East India Trading Company, but Sao Feng sailed right past the official docks and brought the *Empress* to anchor in a secluded harbor just north of the city. It had been a long trip, but Jack thought it wasn't so horrible, what with Lian and Park around.

From the quarterdeck of the *Black Pearl*, Jack watched his crew tie up alongside the junk and surveyed the welcoming party waiting for them.

The pirates at the end of the dock were as menacing and stone-faced as the ones on Sao Feng's ship. But instead of the dragon symbol that all Sao Feng's pirates wore, these pirates wore blue robes with Lions emblazoned in silver thread. Jack wondered when the brothers had chosen their animals. He thought he'd feel rather threatened, too, by a brother who chose something like a dragon to represent him. Now, a nice *dragonfly*, that'd be different. Much friendlier.

Sao Feng descended from his ship like an

emperor returning to his palace. Although the pirates in the lion robes were clearly meant to be guards, he treated them like a royal audience, smiling at them majestically and sweeping past them as if unconcerned by their threatening stances.

Jack wished he felt that confident. He couldn't help but notice the very long, very sharp swords they were all carrying. He also noticed that they looked even less pleased to see Jack than most people who knew him, which was saying something.

But he squared his shoulders and sallied bravely down the gangplank with Barbossa, Carolina, Diego, Billy, and Jean. Marcella had wanted to come and pitched a fit when Jack said no, but he was sure that if anyone could ruin the deal he was about to make, it was her. He tipped his hat at the guards as they sauntered by. The pirates closed rank behind his crewmates and stayed on their heels as they marched off the dock, through an immaculately tended garden, and up to an opulent pagoda dripping with silver and jewels. Two large jade lions roared on either side of the entrance alongside large china pots planted with tall green shoots of bamboo.

Sao Feng and his men slipped off their shoes in one practiced movement as they stepped onto the cool marble floor of the palace. Sao Feng cast a meaningful glance at Jack's feet.

"Really?" Jack said. "You think that's wise, mate? Do you know how long it's been since some of these blokes took their boots off?" He leaned forward and whispered. "Especially Barbossa. Don't tell 'im I said so, but hold your noses now, boys."

His first mate had clearly overheard, as he was now glaring furiously at Jack.

"It is custom," Sao Feng said courteously.

"Oh, all right," Jack said. "But don't say I didn't warn you."

There was a long pause while Jack and his pirates wrestled with their shoes, but finally a line of pirate boots stood against the wall. (And to be fair to Jack, he was quite right about the smell.) Sao Feng wrinkled his nose, but turned in a whirl of robes and strode on down the long hallway.

"Nice place your brother's got here, Sao," Jack commented, marveling at the silk tapestries and red lanterns lining the walls.

Sao Feng snorted. "It is all so obvious," he said. "The East India Trading Company could find him at any moment. And then how would he escape? How would he defend this place? Much better to have a secluded lair with ample underground tunnels, close to the heart of the city. Out here everything goes by, and he does not know. There is no one to carry the whispers to him. His spies are pathetically inadequate. Company agents could be sneaking up on us this minute and we would have no idea."

Jack glanced around uneasily. He definitely did not want to run into any East India Trading Company agents. His encounters with them never seemed to go very well . . . a problem that Jack was quite sure was not his fault.

The hallway opened into a palatial throne room. What seemed like hundreds of pirates in blue and green robes stood or squatted around the edges—conversing in low voices, trading goods, gambling, drinking tea, all in subdued voices. Jack couldn't wait for the day he had that many pirates following *him* around!

At the far end of the room, yellow banners emblazoned with red lions hung from the ceiling around an enormous carved-mahogany chair. Seated in the chair was a man who looked like Sao Feng, but with a shorter moustache and beard, yellow robes instead of green, and more of a paunch around his middle. His eyes were just as shrewd and calculating, however. He pursed his lips as the pirates approached his throne.

"Brother," he said slowly. "You have returned. Unscathed. How . . . delightful." His gaze panned across Jack and his crew. "And you brought friends. Charming."

"I brought more than that," Sao Feng said proudly. Around the room, pirates stopped what they were doing to stare at him. Liang Dao leaned forward with a hungry expression.

"The opal?" he said. "You stole it?"

Sao Feng threw back his sleeve to reveal the opal in the palm of his hand. He held it up so the whole room could see it. Sunlight from the windows high in the walls caught the fire within the opal and magnified it so it sparkled brightly like a black star in Sao Feng's hand. A murmur of awe echoed around the room.

Sao Feng waited a dramatic moment until the whispers died down. Then he stepped toward his brother and, in a voice everyone could hear, declared, "I did not steal it. It was given to me. This opal is rightfully mine—and with it I claim the throne of the Pirate Lord."

"What, *now*?" Jack said as the room exploded into a hubbub of noise. "Can't we get my bit over with first, please? Just throw us the vial and we'll nip out the back, leave you lot to it, cheerio."

"No!" Sao Feng said, drawing his sword. "You must fight alongside us to get what you want! Fight, Captain Jack Sparrow! Fight, any pirate who stands with me—all of you who know that I should be Pirate Lord, not my brother. Not Liang Dao!"

"Never!" Liang Dao shouted. "To me, loyal warriors!"

And before Jack could do a thing about it, a pirate in yellow was pointing a very wicked-looking sword at Jack's throat. Jack's crew grabbed their weapons, forced to defend themselves.

Jack gave the sword an alarmed look and moved it away from his throat with one finger. "That's better," he said and leaped into battle with the attacking soldier. "I say," he shouted at Sao Feng as swords clanked and crashed around him. "This is rather unfair. You might have given us some warning that we'd get caught in your harum-scarum coup here!"

"But then you wouldn't have come!" Sao Feng cried over the din with a triumphant gleam in his eyes. He was locked in a struggle with his brother, each parrying the other's sword strokes with ease. "And surely, Captain Jack Sparrow, you would not have wanted to miss a battle as glorious as this?"

"Actually, that would have been all right with me!" Jack called back, ducking under a wild swing of his opponent's blade. "Just so you know for next time!" He leaped over the blade as the pirate swung at his bare feet.

The clash and clang of swords echoed off the walls. Carolina and Diego were fighting back-to-back, practicing the moves they'd learned together on board the *Pearl*. Barbossa leaped behind a column and fired his pistol at any pirate who came near him. Jean and Billy fought bravely, hardly knowing which pirates were friends and which were foes. It seemed like several of the pirates in blue were switching sides to fight for Sao Feng. They could not resist the power of the opal.

Lian and Park threw themselves into the fray, too. Jack paused in his fighting to admire their abilities for a moment. They both whipped the steel chopsticks out of their hair and used them with vicious skill. Their steel-tipped fans sliced and slashed, leaving trails of blood and ribbons of yellow robes discarded on the floor. Jack was very glad they were on his side. When he managed to catch Park's eye, he blew her a kiss.

There was a loud clatter behind Jack as Liang Dao's sword flew out of his hand and skittered across the marble.

"Aha!" Sao Feng cried triumphantly, seizing his brother and hauling him over to the throne. Keeping his sword at Liang Dao's throat, Sao Feng stood on the chair and fired his pistol in the air.

All over the throne room, the fighting stopped.

"It is over," Sao Feng said, indicating his defeated brother at the end of his sword. "I am your Pirate Lord now."

"You tricked me," Liang Dao snarled, his gaze fixed on the sharp tip pressed to his jugular.

Sao Feng shook his head gravely. "That is

what a pirate does, Liang Dao. You are no good at it—and that is why I should be a Pirate Lord instead." He reached down and yanked a cord necklace off Liang Dao's neck. Holding it up, he announced, "The Piece of Eight is mine!"

A great cheer went up from all the pirates. Jack noticed that several of the pirates in blue were hurriedly stripping off their lion robes and cheering as if they'd been on Sao Feng's side all along.

"Kill me," Liang Dao growled. "You have disgraced me, brother. At least show me enough respect to not make me live through the humiliation of this day."

"You do not deserve to die," Sao Feng said. "You will live, but in disgrace."

"Ahoy, your nibs!" Jack said, drawing Sao Feng's attention to him. "Do you think we could spare a moment for my reward?" He held out his hand palm up. "The vial, if you please?"

"What vial?" Liang Dao asked, struggling as two pirates came up and tied his arms. "What has my lying brother promised you?"

"The uh—the vial of Shadow Gold—don't tell me . . ." Jack trailed off. The answer was clear from the smug look on Sao Feng's face.

"Oh, there's no Shadow Gold *here*," Sao Feng said. "My apologies; did I give you that impression?"

"You bloody well did," Jack said evenly.

Sao Feng laughed maniacally.

"What about the Pirate Code?" Carolina cried. "Where is your sense of honor? You made a deal!"

"I did," Sao Feng said calmly. "And I will keep my promise. We just had to make this brief detour along the way."

"Sounds a bit like my trip 'home' to North Carolina, doesn't it, Jack?" Billy said, glaring at his captain.

Jack drew his sword. "Well, then. If you can't help me find the next vial of Shadow Gold—"

"But I can," Sao Feng said. "We both know another Pirate Lord who is certain to have one. And only I can take you straight to Mistress Ching."

CHAPTER NINE

Naturally, Jack was still very suspicious, but before he could attack, the new Pirate Lord of Singapore spoke again.

"I will explain," Sao Feng said. "My brother has been planning a meeting with Mistress Ching for several months. The threat of the East India Trading Company has grown very strong in our waters. A new man, Benedict Huntington, runs operations from Hong Kong, and he is ruthless when it comes to pirates. Something must be done to stop him, and we believe perhaps the time has come for a joint effort."

All the pirates in the chamber, no matter what region or crew they were from, snickered at the words "joint effort." It was impossible to imagine pirates cooperating.

"Silence!" Sao Feng commanded, and the sheer power of his voice caused the room to fall silent again.

Sao Feng turned over his new Piece of Eight in his hands. "Of course, Liang Dao's foolish idea was to betray Mistress Ching at the meeting, so he could seize control of her fleet. As if a weakling like him could accomplish such a devious plan!"

"I'm still right here," Liang Dao pointed out grouchily from behind the wall of guards that surrounded him.

"*I*, on the other hand, am bold and clever enough to pull it off, if I choose to," Sao Feng said, ignoring his brother. "But for now I intend to go to Hong Kong for the meeting and decide once I have seen her in person." He smiled down at Jack. "You may accompany me, if you wish."

"Why should I trust you?" Jack demanded.

"You shouldn't," Sao Feng said with a shrug. "But if you would like to find your own way to Mistress Ching, go ahead."

Jack fumed. He thought and thought. He was not used to being tricked by other pirates. Normally he was the one doing the tricking. He liked it much better that way.

"Give me your word that you will not warn Mistress Ching that we want her vial," Jack said. "I would rather get it in my own way, thank you very much."

"Certainly," Sao Feng said. "You may proceed however you wish once we reach Hong Kong."

"Why Hong Kong?" Diego asked.

"It is considered somewhat neutral territory between here and Shanghai," Sao Feng answered. "And that is where this Benedict Huntington is stationed. If we can find a way to take him out while we are there, we will."

Lian and Park were making eyes at Jack from behind their fans. Jack cleared his throat. "Sao Feng, I request that one of your pirates come aboard my ship for the journey between here and Hong Kong, to ensure that you do not attempt to fool us again."

"Oh, yes?" Sao Feng said, narrowing his eyes.

"Yes," Jack said. "And you can choose who. Anyone but those two." He pointed at Lian and Park.

"Ah, my deadly attendants," Sao Feng said proudly. "I will agree to your request—but you must take Lian and Park."

"No!" Jack said with melodramatic intensity. "Anyone but them!"

141

"I insist," Sao Feng declared.

"Oh, all right, if I have to." Jack said. Sao Feng turned to his brother, and Jack winked at the warrior women behind his back. Now at least the trip to Hong Kong would be more interesting.

*K*nock. *Knock. Knock.*

"Go away!" Jack shouted from inside his cabin. "I'm not here! No one home!"

Knock. Knock. Knock.

"Sorry, not interested! Already have one!" Jack called again.

Knock. Knock. Knock.

Jack sighed. From the determined, slow tenor of the knocking, he had a pretty good idea who it was.

He cracked open the door to his cabin. "What is it, Alex?"

The zombie blinked for a few moments. His

loose bits of skin flapped unattractively in the breeze as the *Pearl* skimmed along the waves, following the *Empress* to Hong Kong. Behind him on the deck, Carolina and Diego were practicing their sword fighting in the sunshine, while Marcella watched from the railing with a scowl.

"I have a message from Tia Dalma, Captain Jack Sparrow," Alex said finally.

"Ooooh," Jack said. "Tell her she *just* missed me. Better luck next time." He started to close the door, but Alex put his foot in the way. There was a very disturbing squishing sound. Jack didn't dare look down to see what that was all about.

"Tia Dalma says you are not being honest with the Pirate Lords, Captain Jack Sparrow," Alex intoned.

"Well, of course I'm not," Jack said. "That wouldn't be very piratey of me, would it?"

"She says you must warn them about the Shadow Lord, Captain Jack Sparrow."

"Listen, mate," Jack said, trying to edge away from the zombie, "this is a lovely chat, but could we finish it later? I'm a little—"

"The Pirate Lords must be warned, Captain Jack Sparrow. They must be ready when the Day of the Shadow comes."

Jack froze. On deck, Carolina caught Diego's arm and turned to listen.

"Come again?" Jack said, trying to sound casual. "Day of the what now?"

"The Day of the Shadow is coming, Captain Jack Sparrow," Alex said intently. "All the Pirate Lords must fight it together."

"Ah, well, that's where you're confused, my good man. Pirate Lords never do anything *together*. Make a point of it, in fact. If you catch one Pirate Lord doing something, the other eight will find eight different ways to do eight opposite things. That's just the way it's always been."

Jack waved his hands flippantly, but that phrase had chilled him to the bone. How did Tia Dalma know what his nightmare had told him? What did "Day of the Shadow" mean? Most important, how soon was it coming, exactly, and where could Jack hide from it?

"Alex," Carolina said, interrupting their conversation, "what's the Day of the Shadow?"

"A good question, love," Jack said. "How about you two go ahead and discuss, and I'll get back to my massage." He started to close the door again, but this time it was Carolina who firmly barred his way.

"This is important, Jack!" she said.

"*Captain* Jack Sp—!" he began, instinctually.

"If the Shadow Lord is planning something, we're the only ones who can stop it!" Carolina cried, cutting him off.

"Oh, I don't know about that," Jack said. "I'm sure there are plenty of capable hero types out there who'd love to handle this for us. At least five or six of them, I imagine."

All Jack really wanted was the next vial so he could get healthy again. Fighting a great big Shadow Lord and his army was not exactly his priority.

"The Day of the Shadow is when the Shadow Lord will rise," Alex droned, "and all the world will be crushed beneath his boots."

"Charming," Jack said. "I can't wait. May I go now?"

"We have to tell Sao Feng," Carolina said. "And Mistress Ching!"

"Listen, darling, why don't you leave the captainy decisions to me and go back to sword fighting," Jack said. "I'll just go in here and think very hard about all this, um, important stuff until I come up with a brilliant solution.

All right? Here I go—thinking hard!" He managed to shove her aside and slam the door before she could stop him.

"Diego, we might have to take matters into our own hands here," Carolina said in Spanish.

"You don't think we have enough to worry about?" Diego responded, also in Spanish. "With the whole Spanish navy still out looking for you?"

"This is much more important than that," Carolina answered. "The fate of the world could be at stake."

"Well, *I say*," Marcella declared loudly, "Alex, don't you think it's *incredibly rude* when people *deliberately* exclude you from a conversation by talking some *stupid other language*?" The zombie blinked at her, then shambled off to the galley without responding. That didn't stop Marcella. She flounced up to Diego and Carolina, put one hand on her hip, and glared at the Spanish princess. "This is an *English* pirate ship, missy. *Try* to remember that."

"I'm going to the crow's nest," Carolina said to Diego, still in Spanish. "But good luck with *her.*"

Diego's expression clearly said, "Don't abandon me!" but Carolina grabbed the nearest ratline and began climbing the ropes with nimble hands and feet. Soon the hubbub of the ship and the gentle swish of the waves were fading below her.

It was obvious to Carolina that Jack needed help dealing with the menace of the Shadow Lord. If he wouldn't admit that, then someone else would have to figure it out for him.

And there's a funny thing about princesses: once they decide something needs to be done, you'd better believe it's going to happen.

CHAPTER TEN

Storm clouds hung low over the city of Hong Kong, casting a gloomy pall over the normally bright temples and colorful flower markets. Two caped figures strode through the winding gray streets, keeping their faces hidden. But if they intended to conceal their identities, they were not succeeding. Almost any citizen of Hong Kong could recognize the pure white woolen cloak of the figure on the left, or the shimmering emerald satin of the one on the right.

The green hood shifted as the woman underneath it glanced down a dark alley, then turned back to her husband.

"I thought I saw someone running away down that alley," Barbara Huntington whispered, pointing a bloodred fingernail. "What if it was a pirate? A dirty, slithering—"

"No pirate would dare walk these streets now," Benedict Huntington answered, pulling his ermine hood down further. Despite the humid Hong Kong heat, he was covered head to toe, and he seemed determined to hide his face from the sun even more than from the people around him. "My agents patrol every inch of this city day and night. They have strict orders to run any pirate through, without warning if necessary. There is no mercy for pirates here."

"Splendid," Barbara said breathily. "But

how will they know who the pirates are?"

"I have trained all the Company agents impeccably," Benedict answered. "They can spot a pirate on sight. It's not difficult, my dear. As you say, the smell is often the first sign."

The couple rounded a corner and came face to face with a troop of seven East India Trading Company agents, who were wearing the dark blue uniforms Benedict had assigned to them and marching in single file down the street.

"You see?" Benedict said to his wife. "My agents are everywhere. No pirate would dare try to sneak past them! Report, soldier," he said to the leader of the troop.

"Sir!" the man said, snapping to attention with a salute that wasn't quite as polished as Benedict would have liked. But he didn't want to criticize the men in front of his wife, after he'd spent so much time praising them to her. So he decided to overlook the sloppiness—for now. At least the polished gold buttons on the man's tunic gleamed the way they should. He peered at the agent.

"What on earth do you have wrapped around your face?" he asked. The agent's eyes peered out between a traditional three-cornered Company hat and a strange sort of bandanna wrapped around the lower half of his face. "That's not regulation issue, is it?"

"Very sorry, sir," the agent said with an apologetic bow. "You see, I'm quite ill—really quite horribly ill—and I didn't want to spread it to the other agents. Precautions seemed wise, sav—um, if you can comprehend that."

"It doesn't look at all proper," Benedict said, reaching toward the man's face. "I think we can risk a little contagion for the sake of order. What do you have, exactly?"

"Er—" the man said, leaning away from Benedict's fingers. "Leprosy! Yes, most definitely leprosy. Bits of me falling off all over the place. Quite disgusting, really."

Benedict recoiled. "Don't we have distant, quarantined islands where we stash our lepers?" he asked in disgust.

"Yes, sir. On my way there right now, sir," the agent said, nodding agreeably.

"We're escorting him," said another of the agents in an oddly high voice. And—surely that wasn't a *Spanish* accent?

"And keeping an eye out for pirates on the way!" said another, pushing back his hat so some of his red hair escaped. "We won't let any of that scurrilous sea scum get by us, no sir!" He clicked his tall black boots together.

"Long live that spirit!" Benedict said with vicious delight. "Just as I was saying to Barbara, as long as you boys are on the case, I am sure there's not a pirate anywhere in the city of Hong Kong. We'll gut any blackguard who dares set foot in our town. As I promised: nothing for you to worry about, dear," he said, patting his wife on the shoulder.

"Hmmm," she said, her green eyes glittering as she studied the agents.

"Well, we'd better get on," said the first agent, pulling his hat down to cast more of a shadow over his face. "Wouldn't want my nose to fall off while we're standing here, would we? Very messy."

Benedict shuddered. "Yes, yes, on your way. Keep up the good work, lads!"

The troop marched away. He watched them go, admiring how carefully they checked the alleys around them and scrutinized each passerby.

"Admit it," he said to Barbara. "You're impressed, aren't you?"

"Hmmm," she said again.

"Yes, they're very diligent in their duties," he

said. "I've got them all whipped into shape. They've seen the punishment they'll face if they fail me."

"You don't allow women to become East India Trading Company agents, do you, Benny?" Barbara asked.

"Certainly not," he said. "You're the only woman I've ever met who's even half as clever as a man."

Barbara decided to ignore that remark, knowing perfectly well that she was at least five times as intelligent as her husband. "Because four of those agents seemed awfully feminine, including the one with the leprosy, don't you think?"

"They're just young," Benedict said dismissively, waving one white-gloved hand. "I like to start the training early. We'll turn them into big, strong men in no time, don't you worry. Now let's get on to this meeting—I'm sure our mystery informant doesn't want to be kept waiting."

Barbara's shrewd gaze followed the agents as they marched away.

"**W**hew," Jean said, mopping his brow with a regulation issue Trading Company handkerchief. "That was *much* too close, if you ask me."

"Leprosy?" Billy said to Jack. "Are you daft?"

"It worked, didn't it?" Jack said from behind the bandanna, sounding flustered.

"You know what else would have worked?" Billy said. "Shaving your beard so you could look like a real agent instead of a scruffy pirate!"

"Never!" Jack said. "Get rid of my lovely beard for a tiny stroll like this? Do you know how long it took me to get it just right? *You're* the one who's daft if you think that's worth it.

It's bad enough I had to leave my excellent hat behind on the *Pearl*. This one isn't half as nice. And it smells funny."

"That's because it smells *clean*," Billy pointed out.

"I like Jack's beard," Lian murmured from the back of the line, glancing around watchfully.

"Me, too," Park agreed with a giggle. "It is very handsome."

"Thank you, ladies," Jack said, preening. "My thoughts precisely."

"Ew," Carolina said. "Not to quote Marcella or anything, but—gross."

"I still don't understand this plan," Diego said. "Why did Sao Feng send us on ahead? Where did he get these outfits anyway?"

"Stop worrying, lad," Jack said cheerfully. "We'll find him at the meeting place. It's just safer to travel through the streets this way. Makes sense to me. You're just not used to thinking like a pirate yet. And besides, we left Barbossa to keep an eye on him."

"Right. I feel much better," Diego muttered. He suspected that the first mate would take any opportunity to sail off with the *Pearl* if he had half a chance. Although perhaps he wouldn't do it while Marcella was on board. Regular Marcella was bad enough; abducted Marcella would probably be as furious and bad-tempered as a wet cat with its tail on fire.

The group had reached the seedier part of town, where dilapidated shanty houses leaned close together and tiny rivers ran along the gutters. A smoky, sickening smell came from several of the darkened homes where dirty curtains were drawn across the windows to keep the opium smoke in. Several barefoot children in ragged clothes were chasing a dog through the street. The children stopped to watch the newcomers with expressions of hostility and suspicion that were well beyond their years.

A misty rain began sprinkling from the clouds as the pirates stopped to consult the map Jean was carrying. Hunching their shoulders against the dreary drizzle, they huddled in a circle, squinting at the parchment. Diego made sure he was next to Carolina, close enough to share his warmth with her. Her hair was neatly tucked away under a Company hat, but she still looked so beautiful to him that he couldn't believe the British couple hadn't recognized her instantly as royalty. She caught him watching her and gave him a reassuring smile.

"All right," Jean said in a low voice, using one finger to trace the route Sao Feng had drawn for them. "We're close now. The den should be at the end of this row of shacks." He turned to point down the street and found himself on the very unpleasant end of a silver pistol. At the other end was a Chinese woman with a tight black bun of hair, powder white makeup covering her face, and a distinctly mean look in her eyes.

"Um . . . Jack?" Jean said nervously. "I think we might have a problem."

The others turned around and discovered that they were surrounded. A host of pirates had appeared as if from nowhere, dropping silently from the roofs and popping out of the underground sewers. Now they were all pointing an awful lot of nasty-looking weapons at Jack and his crew.

"Oh, bugger," said Jack.

"Agents of the East India Trading Company," hissed the woman with the pistol. "I'm afraid you have wandered into the wrong part of town . . . and now we have no choice but to kill you."

CHAPTER ELEVEN

"WAIT!" Jack bellowed as Mistress Ching—for it was indeed she, and he could figure that out without being told—clicked back the hammer of her pistol. Jack ripped off his hat and bandanna, revealing his long dreadlocks and braided beard. "We're not Company agents! We're pirates! I swear! Dastardly pirates! Yo-ho, yo-ho! Mangy bilge-rats! I love rum! Um—ask me anything; I guarantee I'll lie to you! Really!"

He waved his arms dramatically at himself. "Pirate!" Wasn't it obvious? No one could be more of a pirate than Jack Sparrow!

One of the Chinese pirates snorted disbelievingly. "A pathetic lie to save themselves. As if any self-respecting pirate would dress like that."

"Haven't you ever heard of a *disguise*, you thickheaded buffoon?" Jack said indignantly.

Mistress Ching stared at him. "That voice—those mannerisms . . . do I know you?" she asked. Her accent was thick, but her English was impeccable, and her entire bearing was commanding and awe-inspiring. Even though she was shorter than most of her followers, it was clear why they looked up to her . . . and why no one ever dared to cross her.

Jack swept his hat down into a formal bow. "Captain Jack Sparrow, Pirate Lord of the Caribbean, at your service," he said. "Not sure if you remember me. But then again, who could forget a face like this? We've met once or twice before. I was much younger then. I think you were friends with my dear old dad. Used to play bridge together or some such. You see, my crew and I here . . ."

"Ah, Jack Sparrow," Mistress Ching said inscrutably, cutting him off. "Yes. That explains a lot. What a *dis*pleasure to see you again."

Jack raised an eyebrow.

"Lower your weapons, but keep them ready," Mistress Ching said to her pirates instead of addressing Jack. "This one is not to be trusted . . . but at least he's not an agent of the East India Trading Company."

"Told you so," Jack said, nodding agreeably.

"Why are you here?" Mistress Ching demanded. "What are you doing on my territory? Have you been spying on me?" She raised her pistol again. "I find it very suspicious that you turn up here on this particular day. Is Liang Dao plotting against me?"

Jack was trying to figure out how best to answer that question when Sao Feng emerged from the shadows of a nearby alley, smiling triumphantly.

"Not in the least, my dear Mistress Ching," he said, bowing low to her with his hands pressed together. His men emerged from the shadows behind him, bristling with just as many weapons as the Chinese pirates had. With them was Barbossa, brandishing his pistol and looking as sullen as ever.

"Liang Dao is a Lord no more," Sao Feng announced. "I, Sao Feng, am now Pirate Lord of Singapore. And in my new position," he went on smoothly, "I merely wished to witness your renowned strength and intelligence for myself. I thought if I sent what appeared to be Company agents into your midst, it would be an excellent opportunity to test your skills. And you passed with flying colors." He bowed again. "My deepest respect to you, madam."

"Oh, that's nice!" Jack protested. "So we were just bait in your little trap?" He paused for a moment. "Actually, that's quite clever," he admitted ruefully.

Mistress Ching glanced around the now-deserted streets. Everyone who wasn't a pirate had fled indoors at the first sight of pistols and swords.

"Let us adjourn to our meeting place," she said, gesturing up the street. "It is not safe out here, even for the strongest among us." As she turned, Jack caught a glimpse of something shimmering in her robes. She was wearing the vial of Shadow Gold around her neck! His knees nearly buckled under him. To be so close to what he needed—the shadows pounded inside his head, screaming to drag him into madness before he could reach the vial. He blinked, forcing himself to concentrate.

How could he get it away from her?

Sao Feng fell into step beside Mistress Ching as they walked. "So I understand," he said soberly, "that this Benedict Huntington is a scourge that threatens all the pirates on this ocean. He captured one of my junks last week and hung every last man without even waiting for a ransom to be offered. He even shot the parrot." Sao Feng shook his head. "Something is very wrong with a man who cannot be bought. He must have no head for business."

"He is not the only danger," Mistress Ching said, holding her robes up and out of the filth of the street. "His wife is just as deadly. Perhaps more so. She caught a starving street urchin sneaking into their mansion to steal a handful of rice. No one ever heard from him again. They say she likes to kill things with her bare hands, especially innocent things that cannot fight back." Mistress Ching paused. Then she continued, "She would make a good pirate."

Carolina couldn't help thinking that the Shadow Lord was more dangerous than any Trading Company agent, wife, or pirate. He had the power to destroy the whole world, and that was exactly what he planned to do. She needed to tell Mistress Ching about the Shadow Lord. She opened her mouth to speak, but Diego shushed her, anticipating what she'd planned to do.

"Not yet," he whispered. "Wait for the right moment."

Mistress Ching stopped outside a low doorway. A tattered velvet curtain hung across the closed door, flapping in the misty breeze. The windows were shuttered and the cracks in the walls were carefully sealed, but the sickening smell of opium fumes still seeped through the boards. Carolina wrinkled her nose.

"The meeting is in an opium den?" she asked.

She didn't intend to speak loud enough for the Pirate Lords to hear her, but she had forgotten the legends about Mistress Ching's uncanny hearing. The Chinese Pirate Lord turned to look straight at her.

"The den is only a front, child," she said. "I would never let my pirates fall into that web of sickness and obsession." With a nod to her followers, Mistress Ching led the way through the doorway.

Whether it was only a front or not, the hazy room beyond the curtain was full of very real opium addicts. Hunched shapes huddled in corners or lay prone on low couches, their eyes closed, their heads lolling to the side, and their slow, wheezing breath creating a ghastly background hum. The room was dark, lit only by a red-orange glow from a few paper lanterns, and none of the men they passed looked like real men anymore. Most were covered in thin blankets, their faces turned to the wall as if they had given up on the real world.

Of the few Carolina and Diego could see clearly, long pipes attached to their mouths made them look like curious tentacled monsters, not human at all. A couple men muttered faint curses as a whisper of a breeze came in with the pirates, but they settled back to their pipes and lamps as soon as the door closed behind them again.

In the smoky dimness, it was hard to tell how many people were in the room. It was much bigger than it looked from the outside, so Carolina guessed that there could easily be a hundred men, sprawled on top of each other and pressed close around each lamp, waiting glassy-eyed for their next mouthful of poisonous smoke.

All the pirates, even the fearsome warriors of Mistress Ching's troop, stayed to the center path through the room as if they wanted to keep as far away as possible from the addicts. They avoided brushing against the couches and dirty bare feet that came too close, and most of them stared straight ahead, refusing even to look at the shadowy huddled figures around them. The high tension prickled through the space, and Jack had the distinct feeling that one wrong word might set someone screaming or shooting at any moment. For once, even he kept his mouth shut.

At the far back of the room was a step down into another room. This one was empty of addicts and pipes. The wooden walls were bare, lit by a couple of guttering candles up near the low ceiling. The room contained just two plain wooden chairs. Mistress Ching sat down regally on one of them and arranged her thick robes around her. From her demeanor, it might as well have been a throne.

Jack darted around Sao Feng and sat in the other chair as the pirates filed in and stood around the outer edges of the empty room. Jack crossed his ankles, leaned back, and pronounced, "Well, this is cozy. Who brought the rum?"

Sao Feng loomed over him, glaring. "That is my seat, Sparrow."

"Oh, really?" Jack said. "I thought the chairs were for the Pirate Lords—and since I'm clearly a more senior Pirate Lord than you, what with you being new to the job and all . . ."

Sao Feng seized a handful of cloth at the back of Jack's jacket and lifted him bodily out of the chair.

"I say!" Jack protested, flailing furiously. Sao Feng deposited him on the floor and sat down. Ruffled, Jack brushed off his clothes and stood with his arms crossed between the two Pirate Lords as if that's where he'd meant to be all along. He peeked over at Mistress Ching. The vial glinted in a fold of dark fabric at her throat. If he could sneak it off her neck while she was distracted . . . Suddenly, he realized that she was glowering at him.

"Why is Jack Sparrow here?" Mistress Ching asked Sao Feng, pointing to Jack.

"Is this safe?" Sao Feng asked instead of answering her. He nodded at the opium den. "What if one of them overhears?"

"You saw their condition," said Mistress Ching. "They barely even know they're here. They are the safest men to tell a secret to, because they cannot remember what is real and what is not. We might as well be speaking in front of pigs."

Carolina winced. They were still men—very sick men who needed help and care, not callous indifference. She wished there was something she could do to save them, but the opium trade was a much bigger, more virulent problem than one pirate could solve.

"So tell me," Sao Feng said, folding his hands and leaning forward, "what do you think we can do for each other? I understand your assassins are unparalleled. Why not kill this Benedict Huntington in his own home? Surely the East India Trading Company cannot have too many men like him. If he is replaced with one who might be more easily bribed, one we could reason with . . ."

"'Reason with' meaning 'manipulate,'" Billy whispered to Diego. Diego nodded, but he was watching Jack, who was clearly edging toward Mistress Ching while trying to look subtle about it—and, unsurprisingly, failing. She cast a sharp glance at him and he looked up at the ceiling, whistling innocently.

"It is not so easy as that," Mistress Ching said. "We have tried to assassinate him, but it seems

173

almost as if he is magically protected in some way."

"Magically protected?" Sao Feng scoffed. "He is just a man, like any other. We should not turn him into a figure of sorcery for our easily frightened pirates." He gave his men a hard stare, and they shuffled uncomfortably.

"You may make the attempt yourself," Mistress Ching said coldly. "But I assure you it will fail."

"I can't take this anymore!" Carolina exploded suddenly. All the pirates in the room turned to stare at her. Jack waved his hands frantically, trying to get her to stop, but she stepped forward bravely. "You think this Benedict Huntington—this little mortal man with his business papers and official seals and his nose up in the air—you think *he's* a danger? You have no idea! There's something out there so much bigger, so much more awful and terrifying and deadly and horrible, that even talking about something as meaningless as the East India Trading Company is ridiculous right now!"

"Jack, can you not control your crew members?" Sao Feng said exasperated.

"Obviously not," Barbossa sneered.

"It's probably the opium smoke. Gone to her head," Jack said, waving a finger by his ear as if Carolina were crazy. "Don't mind her."

"No, wait," Mistress Ching said with a frown, silencing them with one gesture of her hand. "What are you saying, girl-child?"

"There is a man called the Shadow Lord," Carolina said, shaking off Jack's hands as he tried to pull her back. She stepped forward and knelt by Mistress Ching's chair. "He commands an army more powerful and vicious and cruel than any this world has ever seen before. We saw what it could do—a whole town, wiped out by fire and destruction.* Not a single soul survived. And his power is only growing stronger. Jack knows it's true! He's heard the prophecy—the Day of the Shadow is coming."

A shiver ran down Jack's spine as he heard those words again, and he could feel the shadows clustering in the corners of his eyes, threatening to block out all the light of the world. But when Mistress Ching looked at him, he shrugged, trying to look like he had no idea what Carolina was going on about.

The way he figured it, if Mistress Ching believed in the Shadow Lord and his army, she might decide to keep the Shadow Gold for herself. She might even drink it before he could! And Tia Dalma had been very clear that Jack needed to drink all seven vials to be cured of his shadow illness. He couldn't risk losing a single

* Carolina is talking about a town in Panama that the *Pearl* sailed past in Vol. 1, *The Caribbean*.

one of them. Generally people only gave up things that they thought were unimportant. So he needed to convince Mistress Ching that the vial around her neck was a meaningless trinket—*not* the only hope for the survival of pirates everywhere! But Carolina was really not helping his little plan at all.

"The Day of the Shadow," Sao Feng murmured thoughtfully.

"When is this Day of the Shadow?" Mistress Ching asked Carolina.

"I don't know," Carolina said. "But it's soon—and we all have to be ready to fight together, or we're all going to die together."

There was an eerie silence as her warning echoed around the small room. All the pirates shifted uneasily, rubbing the goose bumps from their arms.

Mistress Ching stood up abruptly.

"What a supernatural web of words this child

weaves!" she snapped. "A Shadow Lord indeed! We don't have time to slash at shadows and worry about mysterious days that may never come. You might think only of your nightmares, little girl, but we have real problems to face— real flesh-and-blood agents with real muskets and bayonets, who are quite bad enough without you putting shadows in everyone's heads as well.

"No," Mistress Ching continued before Carolina could say anything else. "I don't want to hear anything more of shadows. I am only worried about one thing—Benedict Huntington and his East India Trading Company agents."

"I think that is very wise, Mistress Ching," said an unfamiliar voice. Confused, the pirates looked around to see who had spoken.

In the room of opium addicts, a figure rose from one of the couches, tossing back the blanket that had hidden him from view. His white suit glowed in the lantern light through wisps of curling smoke as he stepped toward the pirates. A cruel smile crossed his unnaturally pale face as more blankets were tossed aside, and one by one, almost all the men in the opium den stood up, revealing a spiky knot of swords and pistols and eyes that were not glazed by opium at all—that were instead glinting with gleeful anticipation of the bloodshed they were about to inflict.

"I think you *should* be worried about me," said Benedict Huntington, his voice as hard and cold as steel. "I think you should be very, very worried indeed."

CHAPTER TWELVE

"**A** trap!" Sao Feng snarled.

"They knew we would be here," Mistress Ching hissed.

Both Pirate Lords leaped to their feet and turned on each other.

"You betrayed me!" they cried simultaneously.

"No," a voice said from the den. One of the agents stepped forward into the light, revealing the face of . . . Liang Dao. He bared his teeth at his brother. "*I* betrayed you."

"Liang Dao," Sao Feng growled. "I was merciful to you. I will not make the same mistake again."

"You know," Jack said, "this really seems like a personal situation, and I hate to be underfoot. How's about me and my crew sally on out of here and leave you all to it? Or just me? Either way."

"Enough talk," Huntington snapped. "Men— a prize to the agent who kills the most pirates! I want them all dead!" He pointed his pistol at Sao Feng and fired.

Lian and Park both threw themselves forward and knocked their Pirate Lord out of the way. The bullet lodged itself in the wall, and pandemonium erupted. Agents swarmed into the room, slashing and shooting in all directions. Pirates leaped into battle with fierce

181

yells, whirling their swords over their heads.

Jack seized one of the wooden chairs and barreled through the crowd, using it as a shield. He whacked a pair of agents over the head with it, knocking them to the floor, and leaped up a step into the antechamber. As he spun and jumped, he suddenly felt a sharp impact on the other side of the chair. He peeked around the edge and saw a wicked-looking axe embedded in the wood. Jack's face lit up with alarm and he ducked behind the chair again. Better in the wood than in his skull!

Backs against the wall, Jean and Billy sparred with three agents at once, kicking in one direction while brandishing their swords in another. Diego tried to push Carolina behind him so he could protect her, but she shoved him aside and punched an agent right in the nose as he lunged toward them. He staggered back with a yell, fountains of blood pouring from his nostrils.

The room was a seething mass of chaos, too small for the number of people trying to swing their swords inside it. Jack ducked between two sparring men and looked around frantically. He couldn't let a thing like this little battle for his life distract him from the *real* battle for his life—and the Shadow Gold. Where was Mistress Ching?

Finally he spotted the Chinese Pirate Lord, slicing fearlessly through the crowd with Sao Feng at her side. They were clearly trying to fight their way over to Benedict Huntington— but the Englishman in white was standing back, chuckling sardonically as his agents fought to protect him.

Jack spun around wildly. Not only was there not enough room to fight properly, but it was far too dark. Jack couldn't tell who was getting struck by his sword. He grabbed one of the opium lamps and smashed the glass. He hoped he could use the lamp to ignite a torch that would make the room brighter.

Instead, the lamp caught on one of the blankets on the couches, which instantly burst into huge flames.

"Oops," Jack said. He picked up the chair again and used it as a battering ram, sweeping people aside as he charged toward the door.

Shouts of terror went up from the pirates and agents as they realized the den was on fire. There was a mass stampede for the exit. The room was now lit up, but it was quickly filling with smoke, which was making it difficult to see once more. It was also becoming difficult to breathe.

Jack was pretty sure he had clambered over a couple of agents, but that was fine with him. Benedict Huntington was the first one to make it outside, but Jack was close behind. As pirates and agents spilled out into the street and resumed their swordplay, Jack and Huntington found themselves facing each other across a water barrel.

Benedict lifted his monocle and studied Jack for a moment, apparently unfazed by the bullets whizzing past their heads.

"Did I hear them call you Jack Sparrow?" he said.

"The very same," Jack said with a jaunty grin. "And you are . . . ?"

Benedict knew that Jack knew who he was. He pressed his lips together. "I have heard of you, Sparrow," he said. "The Company is offering a rather large reward for your capture."

"Ah, well, you're out of luck, mate," Jack said, spreading his hands. "As I have no intention of being captured."

Benedict smiled again. "I believe the reward says . . . dead or alive." A sword suddenly appeared in his hand, a whip-thin rapier as sinister and unfriendly looking as the man himself. With a quick darting movement like a snake, Benedict leaped around the barrel and thrust the point at Jack's heart.

But Jack was already gone. In fact, he seemed to have vanished. Benedict blinked, looking around at the street full of battling pirates.

A whistle came from above him. Benedict looked up and saw Jack standing on the roof of one of the shanties. Diego and Carolina were climbing up the drainpipes to join him, kicking off agents that were trying to grab their feet.

Jack gave Benedict a cheery wave-salute. "Oh, too bad, Huntington. But believe me, this day will live in your memory forever—as the day you came *this close* to catching the famous Captain Jack Sparrow!" With a grin, he turned and leaped to the next roof. Diego and Carolina followed, jumping from rooftop to rooftop and disappearing down the street.

"After him!" Benedict bellowed to his agents, his face paler than ever with rage.

Jack trotted along the peaks of the roofs, windmilling his arms out to the side for balance. "That didn't sound quite right, did it?" he called back to Diego.

"What?" Diego said breathlessly, checking to make sure Carolina was still behind him.

"My exit line. I think it needs work." Jack squinted, musing. "You'll never forget this day—this glorious day when you *nearly*—no, that's not right either. Hmmm."

"Jack, look out!" Carolina yelled. Jack ducked, and a bullet flew over his head.

"Thanks, love!" he cried, and ran on.

"Did you see that?" Carolina said to Diego. "I think that was Barbossa who fired at him! But maybe I'm wrong . . . it's so foggy, and there are so many people down there—"

"I wouldn't be surprised if it were," Diego said. "I don't trust that man." He took her hand and they ran faster, trying to keep up with Jack.

"We need to find Mistress Ching!" Jack shouted. He stopped and shaded his eyes, peering through the misty rain and fog at the tumult of the battle below them. The fighting was beginning to spread to the surrounding streets. The row of rooftops ended at an open square, which was surrounded by taller houses. Jack peeked over the edge of the last roof and frowned.

"I don't like the look of that," he said, pointing to the center of the square. Set up right in the center, where anyone in the square could see it, was a scaffolding with three hangman's nooses swinging in the wind. It seemed clear they were ready and waiting for the three Pirate Lords.

"Look!" Diego said, grabbing Jack's arm. Right below them a trio of agents was battling one pirate. It was Mistress Ching!

"She's amazing!" Carolina said in awe. "I wish I could fight like that."

The Chinese Pirate Lord was a whirl of flashing steel and flying silk robes. She slashed at one agent, then turned and did an astonishing flying somersault over the heads of the other two. Trapping all three of them against the wall of the house that Jack was standing on, Mistress Ching laughed triumphantly, holding her sword aloft.

Suddenly a movement in the crowd caught Carolina's eye. It was Liang Dao—and he was sneaking up on Mistress Ching! A knife gleamed in his hand.

"No!" Carolina shouted. Without stopping to think, she hurled herself straight off the roof of the house.

"Carolina!" Diego cried, terrified.

The Spanish princess twisted in the air, spinning her leg around to kick Liang Dao in the head as she crashed into Mistress Ching, knocking her out of harm's way. For a moment, Carolina and the Pirate Lord were tangled on the ground in a heap of robes. But Carolina quickly regained her footing, and the two women attacked the agents with such violence that the men had no choice but to flee.

Liang Dao stumbled back up to his feet, clutching his head in obvious pain. The knife had flown out of his hands and landed in a nearby gutter. Blinking and disoriented, the former Pirate Lord of Singapore staggered over to it.

Diego was already hurrying down the nearest drainpipe to get to Carolina, so Jack was the only one left on the roof—and the only one who saw what happened next.

As Liang Dao's fingers touched the knife, Benedict Huntington stepped out of the alley behind him. The Englishman's face was completely emotionless as he drew his sword and skewered his ally in the back.

Liang Dao jerked in pain, then looked down at the blade sticking out of his belly with a surprised expression. The sword slid slowly out again, and Liang Dao fell to the cobblestones, blood spreading between his hands where they were pressed to his stomach. He managed to roll onto his back so he could see his killer. His face expressed disbelief, horror, and confusion.

"You—" He gasped. "But I—we agreed—we made a deal. . . ."

Benedict whipped a snowy white silk handkerchief out of his vest and meticulously wiped all the blood off the blade of his sword, pulling it slowly through the cloth.

"I do not make deals with pirates," he said icily.

Dropping his bloody handkerchief on Liang Dao's chest, Benedict Huntington strode away without a second glance.

CHAPTER THIRTEEN

Mistress Ching pushed Carolina away with the force of twenty men. To Carolina's surprise, the Pirate Lord was clearly furious.

"How could you do such a thing?" Mistress Ching spat. Her fists were clenched and black hairs were escaping from her normally lacquered hairdo. "How could you dishonor me in this way?"

"Dishonor you?" Diego said, dropping from

the drainpipe beside them. "Carolina saved your life!"

"I did not ask her to!" Mistress Ching roared. "How *dare* she!"

Diego placed a hand on Carolina's shoulder. She seemed uninjured, but shaken by the older woman's fury. Her hat had disappeared in the fighting, she'd thrown off the uncomfortable jacket and vest, and her long dark hair hung in disheveled waves around her loose white tunic. Diego was so relieved to find her intact that he nearly kissed her, but Carolina's attention was on Mistress Ching.

"I'm sorry," the Spanish princess said, her eyes flashing. "I didn't want to see you die. I meant no disrespect. But we won't bother you with our presence anymore. Come on, Diego." The fighting had moved to the other side of the square, where they could see that Jean and Billy were still in the thick of battle.

"You can't go," Mistress Ching said, her voice dripping with anger. "According to the Pirate Code, I am now indebted to you." Her throat seemed to catch on the hated word. "No doubt it was Morgan who came up with that stupid idea. Bartholomew was notorious for killing anyone who tried to save his life. But that is the Code now. And I refuse to let you leave until our debt is settled." She raised her sword as if she were challenging Carolina to a duel instead of offering her a favor.

Jack came sprinting up to them, having over-heard the last few sentences. He stood behind Mistress Ching, waving frantically at Carolina. He pointed to Mistress Ching, then waggled his hands as if he was holding a vial. He jumped up and down, pointing and waggling like a maniac.

"There *is* something you can give me," Carolina said, glancing at Jack, then back at Mistress Ching.

"What is that?" the Pirate Lord demanded. She didn't notice Jack going berserk behind her.

Jack held up an invisible vial, shook it, beamed at it, and then pointed desperately at Mistress Ching's neck.

"Your word," Carolina said. "I want you to promise me that when the Day of the Shadow comes, you and Sao Feng and all your ships and pirates will stand and fight against the Shadow Lord and his army."

Jack's mouth dropped open.

"You have to be ready," Carolina said passionately. "All the Pirate Lords must fight him, or all will die."

Jack smacked his forehead. He shook his head, clutching his hair in despair. The effects of the last vial of Shadow Gold had almost completely worn off and he was having sporadic shadow attacks. He never knew when the next one might hit.

Mistress Ching regarded Carolina with piercing dark eyes. "You really believe in this Shadow Lord, then?"

"It's all true," Diego said. "We all saw what his army did. That's why we're here—to warn the other Pirate Lords."

Jack made a face that clearly said, "Oh, that is most definitely *not* why we're here!"

Mistress Ching nodded and held out her hand to Carolina. "Very well. I will do as you request. It is not a difficult request to honor—be ready to fight when something attacks me? I think I can manage that."

"Thank you," Carolina said fervently, as she and the pirate she idolized bowed to each other.

"Oh, and one more little, tiny thing, not really important at all, hardly worth mentioning," Jack interjected, separating their hands as he stepped between them. "If we could just have that boring little trinket around your neck, that'd be terrific. It really doesn't suit you anyway," he added, reaching for the Shadow Gold. Right there—right at his fingertips—his vision blurred as the shadows rushed to his eyes, fighting to stop him.

Mistress Ching batted his hand away. "My debt is repaid. I don't have to give you anything." She lifted the vial between two fingers and let the Shadow Gold roll slowly up and down. "Besides, I like to look at it. It's like someone trapped the moon goddess in glass."

"But—but it's so garish!" Jack said, pulling his mouth down disapprovingly. "All shiny and bleeaaagh. It doesn't go with your really quite striking beauty at all."

Mistress Ching patted her hair with a small smile, as if even she could feel the charms of Jack's flirting. "I have a proposal," she suggested. "I will duel you for it."

As much as Jack liked dueling, with all its

opportunities for clever fisticuffs and even more clever escaping, he certainly didn't like the idea of dueling while shadows pulled at his hair and anchors weighed down his chest. Especially with one of the greatest swordswomen in the world. But he had no choice.

"All right," he said, drawing his sword. Mistress Ching drew hers with a delighted gleam in her eyes.

"This duel does seem somewhat unfair, though. If you win, you receive the Shadow Gold. But if I win . . ."

"You get her," Jack said, grabbing Carolina by the arm and pulling her forward.

"I do not need sycophants in my fleet. No, Jack Sparrow, if I win, I receive something far more valuable—your designated Piece of Eight, which makes you a Pirate Lord."

"Oh, come on, Ching, you already have one. Is there really such a need to be so greedy?

Besides, what would two Pirate Lord Pieces of Eight make you? A Super Pirate Lord?"

"We duel now. And we duel to the death!" she shouted, lunging at him.

Jack's eyes popped. Then he flinched, drawing his sword in response to Mistress Ching's attack.

"To the death?!" Carolina cried in horror. "No! No death! Neither of you! Don't you dare kill each other!" She stamped her foot.

But Jack and Mistress Ching weren't listening. Their swords clashed and clanged as they battled each other across the square and up onto the scaffolding.

Jack could feel himself getting weaker. Mistress Ching kept driving him backward— back and back, up the steps toward the eerie swinging nooses. His legs felt weak and his breathing was unsteady. His sword felt like it weighed as much as he did. He could barely block her blows, let alone get any of his own past her blitz of parries and thrusts.

"Your father has wronged me. Many times," Mistress Ching shouted angrily.

"Yeah, that's what mom always used to say, too," Jack said.

"I wish I could see his face when he finds out I killed his son," Mistress Ching hissed, her blade slicing through the air right beside his left ear.

"Oh, is that what this is all about? Revenge on dear old Dad? Don't be so sure that'll work," Jack said. "Kill me, and he'll likely be delighted."

Mistress Ching drove him to the center of the scaffolding. Jack jumped as something brushed against his shoulder. At first he thought it was one of his shadow creatures—but then he felt the scratch of hemp rope against his cheek and realized it was one of the nooses. Wrapping his free hand in the loop, he took a running leap and swung out of reach of Mistress Ching's next jab. Swinging back across the scaffolding, he blocked her sword with his and she jumped back.

"Childish antics!" she barked. "This is not real swordplay!"

"I'm sorry, is there a pirate swordplay rule-book somewhere?" Jack asked, swinging past her once again.

The wooden beam above him creaked ominously. The nooses were made for hanging, not swinging. He couldn't be sure how long it would hold. Using his momentum to drive the rope forward and then pumping with his legs to push himself sideways, Jack swung out in an arc and back toward the scaffolding. Only now he was swinging out instead of straight, and the post at the end of the scaffold was right in front of him.

Mistress Ching stepped forward, ready to skewer him the moment he hit the post. But Jack lashed out with one foot, kicking her in the chest. She fell back, knocked off balance, and Jack let go of the rope, dropping to his feet right at the edge of the scaffold.

Right beside the lever that controlled the trapdoors.

"Sorry about this," Jack said, pulling the lever. The trapdoor below Mistress Ching fell away. With a shriek, she plummeted through the opening, dropping her sword on the scaffold as she fell.

Jack leaped to the ground. By the time Mistress Ching had recovered enough to crawl out from under the scaffold, he had his sword pointed at her throat.

"The vial, if you please," he said, holding out his hand.

"Don't kill her!" Carolina cried.

"Don't you *dare* save me again!" Mistress Ching snapped at her.

"She's not," Jack said. "I'm not going to kill you anyway. Because then you wouldn't be able to repay your debt to Carolina, would you? So you see, by this impeccable logic, you can't let yourself die, or else you'll go to your grave with terrible dishonor on your name."

Mistress Ching opened and closed her mouth, lost for words.

"So just hand over the vial," Jack said. "And we'll be off. Hopefully never to see each other again."

"That I can agree with," Mistress Ching snarled.

Jack carefully placed his blade under the rope that held the Shadow Gold. He came dangerously close to puncturing Mistress Ching's neck. Then with a flick of his wrist, he sliced through the rope and ripped the vial of Shadow Gold from around her neck.

Mistress Ching stood up, grabbed her sword, and stormed angrily away.

"Lovely," Jack said, tucking the vial into his vest. He would drink it as soon as no one was watching him. No need to let word get back to the other Pirate Lords . . . what if they all decided to drink their vials too? Then Jack would really be in trouble. There was only a finite amount of Shadow Gold, and if even one vial was lost or consumed, Jack would never be able to cure himself of the shadow illness. He decided that he'd duck into the nearest doorway and drink it in a minute, in private.

"We did it!" Diego exclaimed, hugging Carolina proudly.

"Yes—well, *I* did it, no thanks to your girl-friend," Jack said, rolling his eyes.

Carolina and Diego glanced at each other uncomfortably, then looked away, their faces flushing.

Jack realized that the square was nearly empty now. The agents had been driven back by the pirates, most of them escaping down the narrow twisting alleys, back to the safety of the wealthier parts of town. Evidently Benedict Huntington had disappeared along with them.

Across the square, Mistress Ching and Sao Feng were bowing to each other. It was only the combined strength of their pirate forces that had defeated the East India Trading Company agents. They had to hope that the combined power of their fleets would be able to do the same thing on the sea.

But if Jack knew pirates—and he knew quite a lot of pirates—this "alliance" wouldn't last very long. One of them would quickly betray the other.

Luckily he would be long gone by then.

"Jean!" Jack called, seeing his friend emerge

from a doorway, supporting Billy, who was limping a little. "Billy! Come on—it's time to say tallyho."

Jack couldn't wait to get back to the *Pearl*. He was glad that Benedict Huntington was Sao Feng's problem, not his. He would feel much better once there was a vast ocean between him and that creepy, pale man.

"Where are we going next, Jack?" Diego asked as Jean and Billy joined them.

Jack held up the vial of Shadow Gold so the others could admire how it glinted, even in the gloomy gray light.

"Well," he said, "it's not hard to guess, really."

"North Carolina?" Billy offered sarcastically.

"Where's the next Pirate Lord?" Jean said, scratching his head. "Isn't there another one in this part of the world?"

"Why, yes there is," Jack said as if Jean had just suggested something marvelous.

"Oh, good," Billy said. "How fortunate for us."

"Who is it?" Carolina asked.

"His name is Sri Sumbhajee," Jack said, beckoning the others to follow him in the direction of the dock. "To the *Pearl* and away, my pirate friends. We're off—to India!"

As they set off down the streets—Billy with a sigh, Carolina and Diego asking eager questions, Jean joking about Indian food—none of them noticed the pale figure spying on them from a nearby doorway.

Strange things happened inside the mind of Benedict Huntington. Behind those calculating eyes, dangerous thoughts were brewing . . . thoughts that blamed Jack Sparrow for his defeat today . . . thoughts that vowed revenge.

"India," he whispered to himself. "Very well. I will see you there, Jack Sparrow."

EPILOGUE

Another darkened hold. The shapes of barrels and boxes loomed in the semidarkness, ropes creaking and groaning as the ship swayed over the waves. A single candle guttered in a hidden corner, shielded from view by stacks of cargo arranged to create a secret den.

Footsteps tiptoed down the ladder from the upper decks. A girl slipped into the shadows, carrying a tin plate of food and a mug of ale.

"I'm sorry," she whispered. "The food here is awful. I brought you the best I could get." She squinted at the candle. "Are you sure that's a good idea? What if someone catches you?"

"I'm not going to sit here in the dark," said the stowaway, taking the plate. "Thank you, Marcella."

Marcella crouched beside the secret den, wrapping her skinny arms around her knees. Her yellow-brown eyes reflected the candlelight strangely. The enormous grin on her face was even stranger—certainly no one on board the *Black Pearl* had ever seen this particular look on Marcella before. It was almost . . . happy.

"I'm glad you're here," she whispered. "You have no idea how horrid this ship is. It's full of horrid, nasty, smelly men who all boss me around. I haven't talked to anyone *civilized* in *forever*. The worst was our cook, Gombo—he was really tall—although at least he smelled like food, not like the awful stink of some of these horrible pirates. But he's gone now, which is why this food is so bad. Ick, I don't even know how you can eat it."

"I need my strength," said the stowaway. "Where did you say we're going again?"

"India," Marcella said, rolling her eyes. "I hear they let cows just wander through their houses there. Can you imagine? I hate cows."

"You should go back up," the stowaway said, handing the empty plate back to Marcella. "They might notice you're missing."

"Oh, no one notices anything around here. And they sure don't notice anything I do," Marcella said, pouting. "Diego would, but that witch Carolina is always distracting him with stupid things like 'practicing sword fighting' and 'sailing the ship,' blah blah blah."

"Come back soon," the stowaway said. "I do so love our talks. I'm glad I'm here, too,

Marcella. If it weren't for you, I would have nowhere to go. Thank you for taking me into your care. Thank you for sneaking me aboard."

"Like that was hard!" Marcella snorted. "These drunken louts wouldn't notice if an elephant came aboard the ship. Which might actually happen in India; with Jack as captain, you never know. Okay, I'll go back up—but I promise I'll be back soon. Let me know if you need anything, ma'am."

"Oh, I'm all right," said the woman in the shadows, leaning back on the pillows Marcella had stolen from Jack's cabin. Her red hair shone in the candlelight. "And Marcella, remember—call me Barbara."

Don't miss the next thrilling volume of

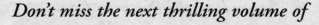

LEGENDS OF THE BRETHREN COURT

The Turning Tide

Rob Kidd

The quest for the Shadow Gold continues! Jack and the crew of the *Black Pearl* find themselves in India—at the mercy of Pirate Lord Sri Sumbhajee. But the crew has an even deadlier threat to contend with—aboard their own ship! You won't want to miss it!

A dim moon rose over the ocean as the wind blew thickening clouds across the sky. Faint shadows were cast up on the island below: huge, black sailing ships, sea monsters, and other things that haunted the midnight waters seemed to cascade over the hills. Few stars were strong enough to twinkle through the stormy haze. The white sands of the beach were swept into little whirlwinds, shifting the patterns on the sand dunes.

A bad night for sailing.

The few respectable citizens of Tortuga stayed snug in their well-guarded houses. Everyone else— buccaneers, swashbucklers, and cutthroats all—was down at the Faithful Bride, drinking ale and rum.

Between gusts of wind from the gathering storm, the noise from the tavern could be heard a half mile away. Laughing, shouting, and the occasional burst of gunfire echoed through the night as drinkers took up a chanty they all knew.

From outside, the Faithful Bride looked like nothing more than an oversize shack. It wasn't even built out of proper wood, but from the timbers of wrecked boats. It smelled like a boat, too: tar and salt and seaweed and fish. When a light rain finally began to fall, the roof leaked in a dozen places.

Inside, no one seemed to care about the puddles on the floor. Tankards were clashed together for toasts, clapped on the table for refills, and occasionally thrown at someone's head.

It was crowded tonight, every last shoddy chair filled in the candle-lit tavern. *I reckon we have enough old salts here to crew every ship in Port Royal*, the Faithful Bride's young barmaid, Arabella, thought. She was clearing empty mugs off a table surrounded by men who were all hooting at a story. Like everyone in the pub, they were dressed in the tattered, mismatched garb common to all the "sailors" of the area: ragged breeches, faded waistcoats, stubbly beards, and the odd sash or belt.

One of them tugged on her skirt, grinning toothlessly.

Arabella rolled her eyes and sighed. "Let me guess," she said, tossing aside her tangled auburn locks. "Ale, ale, ale and . . . oh, probably another ale?"

The sailor howled with laughter. "That's my lass!"

Arabella took a deep breath and moved on to the other tables.

"There's no Spanish treasure left but inland, ye daft sprog," a sailor swore.

"I'm not talkin' about *Spanish* treasure," his friend, the second-rate pirate Handsome Todd said, lowering his voice. There was a gleam in his eye, not yet dulled by drink. "I'm talkin' about Aztec Gold, from a whole *lost kingdom. . . .*"

Arabella paused and listened in, pretending to pick a mug up off the floor.

"Yer not talking about Stone-Eyed Sam and *Isla Esquelética?*" the sailor replied, skepticallly. "*Legend* says Sam 'e had the Sword of Cortés, and 'e cursed the whole island. Aye, I agree with only one part of that story—that it's *legend*. Legend, mate. 'A neat little city of stone and marble—just like them there Romans built,' they say. Bah! Rubbish! Aren't nothing like that in the Caribbean, I can tell you!"

"Forget the blasted kingdom and the sword, it's his *gold* I'm talking about," Handsome Todd spat out. "And *I* can tell you, I *know* it's real. Seen it with my own eyes, I have. It changes hands often, like it's got legs all its own. But there are ways of finding it."

"Ye got a ship, then?" the first sailor said with a leery look in his eyes.

"Aye, a fine little boat, perfect for slipping in and out of port unseen . . ." Handsome Todd began. But then he noticed Arabella, who was pretending to wipe something from the floor with her apron.

She looked up and gave him a weak smile.

She looked again at the floor and rubbed fiercely with the edge of her apron. "Blasted men, spillin' their ale," she said.

Handsome Todd relaxed. But he looked around suspiciously as if the other buccaneers, the walls, or the King himself were listening. "Let's go somewhere a bit quieter, then, shall we? As they say, *dead men tell no tales*."

Arabella cursed and moved away. Usually, no one cared—no one *noticed* if she were there or not. To the patrons of the Bride, she was just the girl who filled the tankards. She had heard hundreds of stories and legends over the years. Each story was almost like being on an adventure.

Almost.

Still, she decided, *not a bad night, considering*. It could have been far worse. A storm often seemed to bring out the worst in an already bad lot of men.

And then, suddenly, the door blew open with gale force.

A crash of lightning illuminated the person in the doorway. It was a stranger, wet to the bone. Shaggy black hair was plastered against his head, and the lightning glinted in his eyes. Arabella held her breath—she had never seen anyone like him before.

Then the door slammed shut, and the candle-light revealed an angry, dripping, young man—

no older than Arabella. There was silence for a moment. Then the patrons shrugged and returned to their drinks.

The stranger began to make his way through the crowd, eyes darting left and right, up and down like a crow's. He was obviously looking for someone, or some*thing*. His jaw was set in anger.

His hazel eyes lit up for a moment: he must have found what he was looking for. He bent down behind a chair, and reached for something. Arabella stood on her tiptoes to see—it just looked like an old sack. Not at all worth stealing from the infamous pirate who was guarding it.

"Oh, no . . ." Arabella whispered.

The stranger bit his lip in concentration. He stretched his fingers as long and narrow as possible, discretely trying to reach between the legs of the chair.

Without warning—and without taking the drink from his lips—the man who sat in the chair rose up, all seven feet and several hundred pounds of him. His eyes were the color of a storm, and they sparked with anger.

The stranger pressed his palms together and gave a quick bow.

"Begging your pardon, Sir, just admiring my . . . I mean *your* fine satchel there," he said, extremely politely.

The pirate roared and brought his heavy tankard down, aiming for the stranger's head.

The stranger grabbed the sack and sidestepped just in time. The mug whistled past his ear . . .

. . . and hit another pirate behind him!

This other pirate wasn't as big, but he was just as irritable. And armed. *And* he thought the stranger was the one who had just hit him in the head with a tankard! The pirate drew a rapier and lunged for the stranger.

It didn't take much to start a barroom brawl in Tortuga.

The Faithful Bride exploded with the sounds of punches, groans, screams, yells and hollers, the clash of cutlasses striking rapiers, and the snap of wood as chairs were broken over heads. All this, in addition to the sound of the crashing thunder and the leaking ceiling that began to pour down on the brawling patrons.

With the giant now otherwise engaged, the stranger hoisted the sack onto his shoulder, turned around and surveyed the scene behind him. What was—for pirates—a fairly quiet night of drinking, had turned into yet another bloody and violent brawl like the others he'd seen in his day. He couldn't resist grinning.

"Huh. Not a *single* bruise on me," he said out loud. "Not one blasted scratch on *Jack Sparrow*."